# WESTWARD THE MONITORS ROAR

# WESTWARD THE MONITORS ROAR

## TODHUNTER BALLARD

WHEELER
CHIVERS

This Large Print edition is published by Wheeler Publishing, Waterville, Maine, USA and by BBC Audiobooks Ltd, Bath, England.
Wheeler Publishing, a part of Gale, Cengage Learning.
The text of this Large Print edition is unabridged.
Other aspects of the book may vary from the original edition.
Set in 16 pt. Plantin.

**LIBRARY OF CONGRESS CATALOGING-IN-PUBLICATION DATA**

Ballard, Todhunter, 1903–1980.
  Westward the monitors roar / by Todhunter Ballard.
    p. cm. — (Wheeler Publishing large print Western)
  ISBN-13: 978-1-4104-2950-6 (softcover)
  ISBN-10: 1-4104-2950-4 (softcover)
  1. Large type books. I. Title.
PS3503.A5575W48 2010
813'.52—dc22                                              2010017704

BRITISH LIBRARY CATALOGUING-IN-PUBLICATION DATA AVAILABLE

Published in 2010 in the U.S. by arrangement with Golden West Literary Agency.
Published in 2010 in the U.K. by arrangement with Golden West Literary Agency.

U.K. Hardcover: 978 1 408 49231 4 (Chivers Large Print)
U.K. Softcover: 978 1 408 49232 1 (Camden Large Print)

Printed in the United States of America
1 2 3 4 5 6 7 14 13 12 11 10

# Westward the Monitors Roar

# CHAPTER ONE

Harmony Jones prided himself on his ability to cook. He was a big man with heavy shoulders and massive forearms more suited to swinging a pick than to juggling a skillet. Yet Harmony had been a cook for his full working life, having started in a San Francisco restaurant when he was only nine years old.

He sang now as he stood before the heavy cast-iron range. His voice was off key and coarsened by the numberless drams of whiskey with which he had cauterized his bull-like throat.

The stove sent off its waves of heat, turning his already fiery face a deeper shade and putting great patches of sweat around the armholes of his undershirt.

The undershirt was his badge of office. No one had ever seen it covered by a shirt. It was of red flannel, and it bulged between the fastening buttons that made a vain attempt to contain his overlarge belly. For Harmony not only loved to cook food, he loved to eat it.

In the long mess hall which occupied all of the big log building save the kitchen, the potboy was dealing out the metal plates from the stack held cradled in his left arm. He was tall for his age, already six feet, a towheaded boy of seventeen with an oversized nose, a receding chin, and a skin still pitted and roughened by acne.

He was not singing. Clarence Donovan found very little in life to sing about. He hated the town, hated the constant roar of the monitors that beat upon his eardrums twenty-four hours a day, and most of all he hated Harmony Jones. There was deep murder in his heart every time he thought of the fat cook. Three times now his narrow hand had crept toward the handle of a French knife lying conveniently on the meat block, tempted by the wide expanse of Jones' back invitingly turned toward him.

Deeper than his hatred was his fear, for Clarence Donovan had been born a coward. He knew this with a burning intensity that kept him awake at night as he turned and twisted on his thin, hard cot. It was something he had fought from first memory. He had run away from it, for the Boston Irish community in which he was born held no place for weaklings or cowards; but what mischance had led him three thousand miles to Dayton, set high in the California foothills, was something he could not determine.

He was here. He ate. He had a place to sleep. He hated. What more was there to life?

He slung the last of the plates onto the long table and moved slowly back to the kitchen. He wished that he could rest. There was no rest. Three pails of unpeeled potatoes awaited the attentions of his knife.

He seated himself beside the table and reached for the largest potato and began to peel. He always picked the largest ones first. They were easier to peel, and they filled the bucket much quicker than the small ones.

His head was bent, and he was stabbing savagely at the potato in his hand, envisioning it to be Harmony Jones' back, when the door on his right opened to admit a swirl of wind-driven sand. He looked up.

The man standing in the entrance was not too tall, not quite as tall as Clarence himself, but there was something arresting about him which made the boy give him a sharp second look. He was somewhere in his early thirties, and the hair showing beneath the low-crowned trailman's hat was white. In contrast, the eyes searching the room with a darting glance were almost black.

He stood for an instant poised on the threshold as if ready to leap backward, then, reassured by what he saw or did not see, he came on into the room.

The wind sucked in after him as if loath to let him escape it, and he used the heel of his boot to kick the door shut, never taking his eyes from the room.

Harmony Jones worked at the long serving table. The table was scrubbed white, for Harmony's kitchen was always the cleanest place in camp. He did not hear the door open or become aware that the man was in the room until he spoke.

"Got a spare piece of meat?"

Harmony turned then. He swore, and there was no man in Dayton who could outswear Harmony when he put his mind to it.

"Ghost Merrill." He dropped the cleaver he had been ready to swing and caught the smaller man by both arms. "Where did you drop from?"

Gordon Merrill smiled his small, cool smile. "From Grass Valley, courtesy of a horse's back, and a rather bony back it was. I smelled your cooking a mile down the road. There's no mistaking a Jones stew. It fills the air with an odor that could only come from a polecat dead a week."

Harmony roared. He clamped an arm about the breadth of Merrill's shoulders, but the white-haired man pushed him away.

"You paw worse than a woman, Harmony. Keep your singing and your big hands to yourself and gimme a cup of coffee."

Jones brought coffee for both and sat down across the table from Merrill. They had not seen each other in three years, but it was characteristic of both men that there was little conversation.

Jones said finally, "Where you been?"

Merrill's shrug was deprecating. "South America, Africa, Australia."

The cook absorbed this information without a change of expression.

"Like them?"

"Not much."

"Going to be here long?"

"Don't know." Merrill finished his coffee. He stood up. "Be seeing you." He moved to the door and went out again into the blustery late afternoon.

The boy hunched over the pails of potatoes stared after him. Africa, South America, Australia . . . names. Names he had barely heard, but for him they held an abiding satisfaction. He turned curious eyes toward

11

Harmony Jones and broke one of the rules he had imposed upon himself, not to speak without first being spoken to.

The cook was still seated at the table. His wide hands were palm down on the table's smoothness, the tufted black hair matted on their backs making them look larger than they really were.

"Who is he?"

Harmony Jones had been daydreaming himself. His mind came back to the kitchen, and he looked around with a start.

"Who? Oh, the Ghost. That's Gordon Merrill. He's one of the best mining engineers this country will ever see."

Clarence Donovan looked at the door. "Why do you call him the Ghost?"

"His hair. You noticed it's white?"

The boy nodded.

"Him and his wife got caught underground at Hawthorne. That was eight years ago. She was pinned down by a timber and he worked three days to free her. He finally got her out, but when he reached the tunnel mouth he realized she was long dead. His hair turned white that night."

The boy was silent, indrawn, picturing in his mind the ordeal Merrill had gone through. He shivered, thinking of the dark tunnel, of the caving roof, of the woman crushed beneath the fallen timber.

And suddenly he had a burning desire to know this man, to talk to him, to confide all the confusing fears which had held him for so long in their grasp.

He rose, leaving the knife sticking in a half-peeled potato, and headed for the door.

"Hey, where you going?" It was the cook. "Come back here and get the skins off those spuds."

"Go to hell," said the boy. He pulled the door open and stepped out into the blowing sunshine.

There the monitors' roar seemed to increase a hundredfold, deafening him, although the pit was a good mile away. He did not know where he was going. He did not know where Merrill had gone, but he did know that he had to find the white-haired man.

# CHAPTER TWO

Park Campbell had been a college professor once, a brilliant man whose subject was history. But there had been a pretty girl in one of his classes, a girl developed beyond her years, and the resulting scandal had driven him from academic halls and sent him swirling like a piece of driftwood from one frontier town to the next.

Sober, he tended business with an air of detached amusement. Drunk, he quoted the names and dates of Roman emperors and bored his listeners with the antics of the early English kings.

Seldom was he entirely sober, and he was not sober now as he watched his latest guest come through the double doors into the semigloom of the hotel's constricted lobby.

In the sense that the company did not own its businesses, Dayton was not a company town. Only the bunkhouses and the mess hall came directly under the control of the mining manager. Nevertheless the company loomed like an octopus over all. Ninety per cent of the labor force worked in the pit, the mill, or serviced the miles of flumes and water ditches which filled the reservoirs at the mountain's crest. Like all of the townspeople, Park Campbell hated the company, but unlike most he realized that without it there would be no town, no business for anyone.

He guessed at once that Merrill was a company man. It was not too difficult a guess to make, since Dayton was far off the main roadways and few men ever drifted here without having some business at the pit.

He reversed the dog-eared ledger and extended the blunt-pointed steel pen and watched the new man inscribe his name in a neat and careful hand. He turned it back, reading *Gordon Merrill, San Francisco,* and said in his professional voice, "Will you be with us long, Mr. Merrill?"

"Don't know."

Merrill had no interest in the man behind the desk. He had sized him up at a single glance, past middle age, frustrated, with the mark of liquor already heavy upon him.

Merrill. Campbell was searching his mind. The name registered — he prided himself

15

that he never forgot a name — and yet he was certain that this white-haired man had never stopped at the hotel before. White hair. That was it. He remembered now, the man who had cleaned up Bodie, Ghost Merrill. His gray eyes were thoughtful as he reached down the key from the hook board and handed it across.

"Number ten. A dollar a night. It's at the end of the hall."

Merrill nodded. He moved back to the stairs, climbed to the second floor, and moved along it to the rear. The room was neither better nor worse than he had expected. He had known a thousand such rooms in a hundred mining camps. The smells were the same — bad, unventilated air, dust, and the cloying odor of past occupancy never entirely removed by proper cleaning.

He raised the window sash, heedless of the blowing dust, heedless of the roar of the giant nozzles in the distant pit. Turning, he tossed the saddlebags onto the bed and was in the act of stripping off his blanket coat when the knock came at his door.

He made a half turn, spinning on his heel, and was facing the door, the coat held back by his elbow out of the way, his hand not more than inches from the butt of the heavy gun which lay flatly against his hip.

"Who is it?"

"Clarence Donovan."

"I don't know you."

"I'm the boy who was peeling potatoes in the mess-hall kitchen."

Merrill relaxed. The coat fell back into place, and its skirt hid the holstered gun. He supposed that Harmony had sent some message.

"Come in."

The door opened and Clarence Donovan stalked into the room. His long legs were like a stork's, too thin except for the knobs at knee and ankle. He shut the door and took off his hat and just stood there, searching for words.

Merrill said, "Well?" his natural impatience riding up into his voice. "Harmony send you?"

"No, sir."

"Then what do you want?"

"I . . . I want to talk to you . . . have to talk to you." The words came out in a rush as if pushed forth by some internal explosive quality.

"You have to talk to me? What about?"

"About me."

"You? What's there to say about you?"

"I'm . . . I'm afraid."

Merrill's laugh was dry, without mirth. "That's a malady the whole human race suffers from, boy. Show me the man who has never been afraid and I will show you a man too stupid to know what life is."

"Yeah, but not like me." The boy came a step forward into the room. "No one's ever been afraid like me. I'm afraid of everything. . . . Everything." His voice rose on the last word until it sounded almost a wail. "Please, Mr. Merrill, you gotta listen to me. You gotta help me."

Merrill sat down on the edge of the sagging bed. He pulled a black, crooked Mexican cigar from his breast pocket and thrust it between his thin lips.

"And just why do I gotta do anything for you? I don't know you. You are the homeliest, most unattractive kid I've seen in a long while. Did anyone ever like you?"

Clarence Donovan shook his head.

"I thought not. Did you ever do anything to make people like you?"

Again there was the shake of the head.

"Why not?"

"Well, I used to try, but everybody made fun of me. I used to hate them all. I could have killed them."

"But you never did."

The boy stared at him, his fish mouth

18

slightly agape. "You mean I should have killed someone?"

"I mean that you've got to have some respect for yourself. People may not take your own opinion of yourself, but they sense it when you are unsure, when you're apologetic. Quit ducking. Stand up and fight."

"I always get licked."

Merrill's thin mouth quirked. "So do we all, Clarence. That's a hell of a name, Clarence. What's your nickname?"

"I never had one."

The man considered the boy carefully, the way he might have examined a horse he was thinking of buying. "Nicknames are important. Sometimes a man tries to live up to his."

"Like when people call you the Ghost?"

The man on the bed was very still. It was as if he had suddenly frozen. No emotion showed in the dark eyes, and his mouth was a hard, straight line broken only where the lips molded around the butt of the cigar. The boy had a sudden perception, alien to him.

"I shouldn't have said that."

"Why not?" Merrill spoke in his flat, toneless voice. "It's the truth. Nicknames make the man or man makes the nickname. It doesn't matter much."

19

"I'm sorry . . . I . . ."

"If you say that again" — there was sudden viciousness in Merrill's voice — "I'll whale you until you can't stand up. The people who call me a ghost are right. I died eight years ago. Now, get out of here."

The boy watched him in a kind of horror, then turned and would have run from the room, but Merrill's command stopped him.

"Come back here."

The boy came uncertainly. Merrill again looked him up and down, then he stood up slowly and pulled back his coat, exposing the well-worn gun in the holster at his hip. His hand moved, and the gun was nestled in his palm, loosely held yet perfectly balanced.

The boy's pale eyes opened, seeming to bug from his head. He was very certain that his last moment on earth had arrived, although for the life of him he could not understand why Merrill had decided to kill him. His mouth opened, but no words came, and his knees were suddenly so weak that he feared they would bend the wrong way.

Merrill saw the look, and there was cold amusement within him, not that evoking fear gave him any pleasure. Whatever else he was, he told himself, he was no bully. He reversed the gun neatly, easily, and extended it butt first to the boy who stared at him still not comprehending.

"Take it."

Clarence Donovan's hand came out timidly, and his fingers closed fearfully around the grip. He stood for an instant, the barrel pointing at Merrill's stomach, then he let his hand fall so that the gun threatened nothing but the floor.

"How's it feel to hold a gun?"

The boy frowned, sensing that the man was trying to get some message across.

"A gun," said Merrill, "makes the littlest man in the world the equal of a giant. Is that right?"

"I . . . I guess so."

"Do you feel any bigger, holding a gun?"

The boy thought about it, then he nodded. "I could kill Harmony. I could blow a hole right through his belly."

Merrill shook his head. "No you couldn't. You pull a gun on Harmony and you'll get yourself killed. A lot of men have managed to get themselves killed because they stuck a gun in their pocket and thought that was the answer."

He paused, found a sulphur match, and lit his cigar deliberately. "There are two things about wearing a gun. A gun is a threat, and only a fool makes a threat unless he's willing to back it up with action. This has got to come from inside yourself, Clarence. It's not something you can fasten around your waist with a cartridge belt. It's something you develop with experience and growth and will power. Give me the gun."

Clarence extended it to him butt first. "It's easy for you to say." His voice was bitter. "You were born this way."

"Was I?" said Gordon Merrill. He said it softly, more to himself than to the boy. "I think not. Now get out of here, but the next time you are afraid just say to yourself, 'I'm not. What can this man do to me . . . hurt me physically? That's not too bad, you recover from a broken leg or arm. What can he do to me . . . kill me? Dying isn't something to be afraid of, this world and our experiences in it are not so precious that we should be afraid to die. What can he do to me . . . destroy me?' But you are already destroying yourself with fear, boy. Think about it. Think about it. But take your thinking elsewhere."

In the dingy, badly lit hallway Clarence Donovan knew a deep, a consuming frustration. Merrill's no different from the rest, he told himself. He doesn't care, he doesn't understand. He doesn't want to give me

22

help. But strangely he was conscious that the bitterness was directed at himself, not at the man.

He continued on down the stairs, muttering to himself under his breath. "I was a fool to expect him to do anything. I've always been a fool to expect anything from the world. Why should anyone do anything for me? Merrill's right there. I never once in my life tried to make anyone like me. I never cared whether they liked me or not. But I do care whether he does, and he doesn't. He doesn't even know I exist."

He stopped muttering suddenly, for Mary Campbell was standing in the lobby, looking up at him.

"Is anything the matter?"

He knew who she was although she had never before spoken to him. He shook his head, finding no words to speak aloud, confused by this sudden intrusion into his jumbled thoughts.

She was large for a woman, with soft light-brown hair that caught highlights from the swinging lobby lamp which she had just lighted. Her face was oval, quiet with an inner repose as if she had made a peace with herself, and there was a certain radiant quality about her, like an aura, that invited the trust of those around her.

Mary Campbell was twenty-six. Want of health had brought her west to live with an uncle whom she had never before seen, and health had twice kept her from marriage, for she had refused to saddle either man with the care of a probable invalid.

At first Dayton had both appalled and fascinated her. It was as foreign to her upbringing and early environment as if she had been abruptly whisked to the moon.

She had seen men die in its streets. She had seen men fight at the Saturday night dances for the sheer animal pleasure of pitting their strength against their fellows.

The carefully tended veneer of life which bound the middle-class society she had known was nonexistent in these foothills. Life and the struggle to preserve it were too close to the surface for Dayton's citizens to waste energy on the niceties with which her people had clothed their behavior in the name of civilization.

Her uncle had shocked her. From her childhood she had heard him referred to in carefully chosen phrases, for to the family his disgrace was as poignant as the day it had happened.

It had been a portion of her surprise and growing awareness and growing up to find him a tired old man, disillusioned but not bitter at all that had befallen him. That he still retained a sense of humor, that he was tolerant of the people around him and amused by his own predicament had been incomprehensible.

But she had come to realize, in the few short months since the Grass Valley stage had deposited her before the hotel, that he was a far more rounded, more solid man than her own father. To her father the church was the final authority. She had been brought up to believe the seemingly basic tenets of the Christian religion as interpreted by her father and his friends; pleasure was wrong, a sin in itself. Theirs was an austere society sitting in judgment on their fellow man.

One of her father's bitterest moments had come when he shipped his only child westward into the care of his dissolute brother. The words were her father's, not her own, but the hesitation with which she had approached Dayton, the uncertainty with which she had faced Dayton, had been borne in utter desperation.

It had been a choice between almost certain death and damnation, and being human she had chosen damnation.

It amazed her now, six months after her arrival, that she had so recently viewed the town and the country and its people with such unreasoning horror. As she told herself now, she had yet to meet anyone with horns. She had yet to be accosted by a man on the street, and she had served breakfast to a murderer while his victim still lay in the dust of the roadway.

Six months ago she could not have faced such situations, but then, six months ago she could barely leave her bed. Strength had returned, and a new tolerance had grown in her, both fed by the warm dry air of the foothill land, by the wholehearted zest for life of the rough men who labored in the pit.

She looked upward at the boy standing above her on the steep steps, and out of her own travail she read the misery in his homely face.

"Come on down."

He came reluctantly. He knew little about women, and he feared them even more than he feared men because they were unknown. He barely remembered his mother, work-worn, strident of voice, bitter of tongue, always, as his father said, carping just because a man stopped at the corner for a bit of a drop with the boys of a Saturday night.

"There is something the matter." There

26

was an insistence about her that would not be denied. "Come into the kitchen and have a cup of tea with me, and tell me about it."

He went, not because he wanted to but because he did not know how to refuse. The kitchen was not as large as the one at the mess hall, but it was equally clean. A Chinaman worked at the stove preparing the evening meal, his pigtail wrapped neatly about his smallish head, his black skullcap not quite covering it. He turned to glance at them and then, with no acknowledgment of their presence, went on with his work.

Mary motioned the boy to a seat at the table. She found the teapot, measured the curled, dry leaves into it, poured boiling water from the kettle on the stove over the leaves. Then she sat down across the table from Clarence Donovan.

"All right now. Tell me about it."

He scuffed the worn floor with the thick sole of his hobnailed shoe. "There ain't nothing to tell."

She thought of herself, of the desperate loneliness of her first few weeks in Dayton, and she said, "There is always something to tell. The trouble is, we find difficulty in putting it into words. Try. Tell me your name."

He told her.

"Your home?"

"Boston."

It sparked a kind of kinship, for her own town was only ninety miles from the Back Bay city. Within moments he was talking to her as he had never been able to talk to anyone in his unhappy life.

Other than geographically their worlds were far apart. She had been brought up to look upon the communities of shanty Irish as interlopers, an uncouth breed that worshiped at another church and, as far as her narrow creed had run, almost another God.

Only in the west, she thought, could she and this boy sit at a table and find a bond in the happenstance that both came from New England. The west was a leveler. Here a man and a woman were what they were, not because of family background but because of their own native ability and personality.

The boy talked on. The dam, once breached, washed out. He told of his childhood, of his running away and heading west, of the towns and places where he had lingered along his route.

And finally he was talking of Gordon Merrill, his voice taking on a note of added excitement.

"If I could be like him . . . so sure of myself, so able to handle everything . . . You feel it when he walks into a room."

She said, "I don't know him."

"You will. Everyone in Dayton will know him. They call him the Ghost."

"The Ghost?"

He told her about the white hair and the mine accident. "I shouldn't have opened my mouth, but you know, he wasn't mad. He said it was all right because I was telling the truth. He said something else that I didn't understand. He said that he was dead."

# CHAPTER THREE

Boris Trueblood had told Gordon Merrill, "You can murder Austin Cleaver for all of me. The man's a fool, and a conniving jackanapes who wears two faces at the same time."

They had been sitting in Trueblood's office in the Market Street branch of the Pacific Central Bank. Outside the big front windows the heavy traffic of downtown San Francisco flowed past: carriages transporting gaily dressed women, delivery carts, slow, laden wagons, and a parade of gentlemanly pedestrians.

"He's robbing us blind, and he can't be doing it alone. He has to have accomplices, and the men who work for him up there will give you no welcome."

Merrill gave no sign of being impressed. The Magnus Mining Company had summoned him home for just this reason. It was not the first time they had sent him in to straighten out a town.

Three days later he was sitting in Austin Cleaver's Dayton office, studying the man across the desk with as empty a face as he had showed Trueblood.

After Clarence Donovan left his room, Merrill washed his face, shaved, and changed to a fresh shirt. By the time he left the hotel the sun was well down behind the western ridges, and the lamps were turned on in the windows of the stores and bars.

The building which housed the local headquarters of the Magnus Mining operations was a two-story brick affair set in the middle of the block, diagonally across the rutted thoroughfare from the hotel. Gordon Merrill crossed the street, ducking between the heavy supply wagons which rumbled past, bearing the endless loads of supplies to feed and equip the town, and came into the entrance of the building.

A wooden staircase led to the second floor. The upper corridor, lighted by a single oil lamp in a wall bracket, was flanked on both sides by the business offices of the mining company, and at the end of the dim hall was an anteroom with an office on either side.

There was a brown-haired girl behind the reception desk when Merrill came in. She looked up, frowning a little, then glancing down at the watch pinned to her shirtwaist above her left breast.

"We close at five. I don't think Mr. Cleaver can see anyone else today."

Gordon Merrill removed his hat. His thick hair glistened whitely in the yellow lamplight and made a startling contrast to his unlined, boyish face. But there was nothing boyish or hesitant in his manner.

"He'll see me." The words had a flat finality which brooked no argument. "Tell him it's Gordon Merrill."

Abruptly there was a change in her smooth, oval face, which looked immature and babylike, a change in the voice that matched her face.

"Oh. So you're Gordon Merrill."

There was an accusation in her tone, as if she blamed him that she had not recognized him. Lights danced for an instant in Merrill's eyes, and his lips seemed thinner for a brief moment.

"What did you expect, a long beard?"

Her face showed her shocked surprise, then the brown eyes filled with hurt as if he had deliberately misunderstood her. She rose and almost fled into the side office, closing the door rather noisily behind her, and Merrill heard the rumble of a man's voice within. Then the door opened and Austin Cleaver came forward, hand extended.

"Gordon. We didn't expect you until tomorrow."

Gordon Merrill managed to ignore the outstretched hand, and his tone was dry irony as he said, "I'm sure you didn't." He walked around Cleaver and into the man's office.

The girl was gathering up papers from the desk. She looked at him across her shoulder, giving him the same half-hypnotized attention with which she might have watched a stalking tiger. Cleaver followed him slowly.

Without turning Merrill said, "Send her home."

Cleaver started, came around Merrill to look closely at him, then the smile which he had been holding firmly on his lips faded and anger came up into the blue steel of his eyes. For an instant it seemed that he would refuse, then he said in a controlled voice, "Run along, Betty. I'll see you in the morning."

The girl looked at him quickly, started to speak, then looked at Merrill and changed her mind. She went out hurriedly, and they heard her cross the anteroom. Then she was gone, closing the hall door a little more loudly than necessary, her footsteps measuring her retreat toward the front of the building.

Cleaver spoke in a tight voice. "Was that necessary, Gordon?"

Merrill crossed to drop tiredly into a chair beside the desk, his unfastened coat falling open and exposing the belted gun.

"When I'm about to call a man a thief I'd as soon say it to him alone."

Austin Cleaver was as big as Merrill and far better filled out. His face was round from good living, and liquor had just begun to spiderweb creases at the corners of his eyes. He had the same smooth skin as Merrill, and there was a small similarity of features, but Cleaver's coloring was blond.

"Be careful what you say, Merrill."

"When have you ever known me to be careful with the truth?"

Cleaver moved forward and stopped behind the desk. "So they sent you here to play God. I've seen you work. I've seen you make men crawl on their hands and knees. But Gordon, I am one man who will never crawl to you."

There was a ghost of bitter amusement in Merrill's tone. "You're still a master of words, Austin. You always could make great speeches on what you would and would not do. But when you got yourself in trouble at White Pine you were glad enough that Boris sent me to bail you out. And glad enough when you were squeezed in the Silver Deuce operation in Virginia City to have us bail you out again. Boris only lectured you. I'd have sent you to jail."

Cleaver's smile was open mockery. "You'd have liked that."

"No," said Merrill. "I don't care. I have no feeling about you, no feeling about anyone. But you've made your last mistake with Magnus Mining Company. I want your resignation by noon tomorrow. I want all of your reports, flow sheets, everything. And I'll warn you. Boris figures that there's as much as a million dollars' worth of gold missing. If I can trace it to you you're going to Folsom, and you're going to stay there for a long time."

"You can't talk this way to me."

"I can," said Merrill without interest. "Do you want to try to stop me?"

Cleaver laughed suddenly. "You want me to go up against you with a gun, don't you? It would give you a chance to settle every-thing. You'd love nothing better than a chance to kill me the way you murdered Tom Spain."

"Another thief," said Merrill calmly. "He

should have remembered the mirror behind the bar before he tried to shoot me in the back."

He stood up easily. "At noon." He walked to the door and spoke without turning. "And this time it will do you no good to drag your tail into Boris' office. He's had enough." He stepped out and closed the door.

He crossed the anteroom and went on down to the street. He felt no elation. Eight years ago this situation would have mattered to him. Tonight it was nothing but a job. Austin Cleaver might be a stranger whom he had never before met.

Behind him, in the office Merrill had just left, Austin Cleaver sat down at the desk, knotted his hands on the surface before him, and stared at them, through them, brooding.

Another thirty days. That's all they needed. Then they would be in control of the Magnus Mining Company, and True-blood and his associates would be gone. Thirty days and the old scores would be evened, and he could take his rightful place in the office at the Ferry Building.

But they did not have thirty days now. They did not have thirty hours.

His first impulse was to have Merrill

killed. But that would not solve the problem, for the men in San Francisco would immediately send someone else.

If only Gordon Merrill were susceptible to reason. Much as he hated the white-haired man he would have included him in his plans rather than see them fail.

But Merrill was incorruptible. A man who wanted nothing, cared for nothing, was a hard man to buy.

What then? Boris Trueblood and the board of directors of Magnus Mining had the utmost faith in Gordon Merrill. If he reported to them that he was studying the situation but that the study would take time, they would never question the message.

The thing was to get hold of Merrill, to hold him somewhere for a month. At the end of the month they would have sufficient stock to elect a new board, one he could control, and that new board was not apt to ask questions about the missing gold, for they would owe their existence to the fact that he had stolen it.

He rose abruptly, blew out the student lamp, and left the office with a swinging step. He was not a man to let worry ride him too much. He was an opportunist who when thwarted in one direction went easily in another.

The Pit was the biggest saloon that Dayton boasted. It had rivals, for a man who worked hard all day needed the warmth and relaxation he could find only in a saloon, but the Pit drew the bulk of the trade and was the choice of the town's leaders.

Cleaver came in to find the deep room nearly deserted, for it was approaching the supper hour. Three miners sagged wearily against the bar, beer glasses at their elbows, idly discussing the prize fight last week in Grass Valley. A single bartender was on duty, absently polishing glasses from the rows which lined the counter of the ornate back bar. Four men played a desultory game of poker at one of the eight tables in the rear.

Jason Comstock, the swamper, was spilling fresh sand into the spittoon boxes. He looked around as Cleaver paused at his side and thrust a silver dollar into his hand.

"Find George Spain and tell him I want to see him. I'll be in the back room. And tell Harry to send me a bottle and two glasses."

He watched Cleaver go on, push open the connecting door, and enter the smaller room which was reserved for the high play games and special guests. The swamper looked down at the dollar resting in his dirty

38

palm. His bearded face was expressionless, but his eyes showed his dislike. He moved over to the bar, motioning to Frank behind the high counter.

"Send his nibs a bottle and two glasses."

The bartender was thin. The Adam's apple on his turkey neck rose and fell above his high starched collar.

"What's he up to now?"

The swamper shrugged, turned away, and lounged out through the bat-wing doors into the darkness of the street.

# CHAPTER FOUR

Coming into the hotel lobby, Gordon Merrill found Mary Campbell behind the high desk, bent over a stack of bills. The lamp above her head threw light on her soft hair, shimmering on it like an aura.

He paused. From the dining room on the right he heard the rattle of dishes and judged that the evening meal was already in progress. But instead of turning that way he continued forward toward the desk. The interview with Cleaver had been distasteful, and the girl made a pretty picture. A moment of chatting with her might put him in a better frame of mind to face his supper.

The girl sensed rather than heard his approach and looked up. She saw the young face, the white hair. She remembered suddenly what the boy had told her and spoke without conscious thought.

"You're Mr. Merrill."

The words caught Gordon Merrill by

surprise. He removed his hat, inclining his head briefly. "How did you know?"

She was at once embarrassed. "I . . . a friend of yours told me who you are."

"A friend?" He searched his mind for possible friends. "Harmony Jones?" The cook was the only friend in this town whom he could think of.

"A boy named Clarence Donovan."

"Oh." Merrill's tone told her more than he intended, and she looked at him quickly.

"I judge that you hardly consider him a friend."

Merrill did something that he seldom did. He hedged. "I barely know the boy."

"You made a terrific impression on him." She put the bills aside and leaned forward against the desk top. The stool on which she sat was low, so that the counter came nearly level with her shoulders. She put her forearms on its edge, crossed them, and rested her chin upon them, looking up at him.

There was an intentness about the girl, a preoccupation with her subject that he found appealing. She was not beautiful. Her face was too thin for that, but there was a flush to her cheeks which deepened the gray of her eyes. He had no way of knowing that this flush was an indication of fever, that she had spent the last four years of her life battling for her existence.

Merrill shrugged. "He's rather a lost soul."

"Completely lost. He told me everything you had said to him."

Merrill raised a questioning eyebrow. "I didn't say much. What is there to say in a case like his?"

"You were very kind."

The word startled him, then he began to laugh. "Kind? You're the first person who's thought of anything I have done in the last years as kind. Ask any man who knows me. Ask Austin Cleaver."

"What has Austin Cleaver to do with this?"

"How well do you know him?"

"He lives at the hotel. He eats in the dining room."

"And I suppose he's made love to you?"

The flush was immediately deeper on her cheeks, and she said in a voice from which all warmth had been squeezed, "That is not a nice thing to say."

"Austin Cleaver is not a nice man. You are a very attractive woman, and I have never known him to overlook an attractive woman."

She straightened, withdrawing her arms from the desk. "Really, Mr. Merrill. I was feeling sorry for you. I don't feel sorry for you now."

"Sorry for me?" He laughed again, but shortly, curtly. "And why should you feel sorry for me?"

"Clarence told me how you lost your wife."

For an instant she thought that the man on the other side of the counter would strike her. She saw the fist clench at his side and sensed a violence within him such as she had never suspected in any man. Then he had control of himself and was saying evenly, "It doesn't matter. Nothing matters, Miss . . . ?"

"Campbell. Mary Campbell." All the flare of anger she had felt against him a moment before was washed away, for she was recalling the boy's words.

Mary Campbell had never consciously hurt anyone, yet there was nothing soft about her. From the time she understood that she had consumption she had kept herself alive as much by will power as by the doctor's help, and it was she herself who had decided to come west to this vaguely remembered uncle. So she did not back away now. Something in this man's face, something in his eyes offered her a challenge which she could not refuse.

"It's ridiculous to say that it doesn't matter. Of course it matters. None of us likes to have a stranger pry into his personal affairs."

"It doesn't matter." Merrill tried to choke off the conversation with deliberate rudeness. "For your information, Miss Mary Campbell, nothing has mattered to me for the last eight years."

"Because of your wife's death. That too is ridiculous."

"It's a word you seem to like." His mouth twisted into what might have been the beginning of a smile, but no expression touched his eyes.

If you meet them squarely, the girl thought, they are the coldest, most empty eyes I have ever seen. They are like shiny metal, without depth. They are indeed the eyes of a dead man. The thought sent a shudder through her, for she had fought death within her own body and knew it for a terrifying enemy.

"I only use it when people say things they don't mean."

"And you've decided that I don't mean what I say."

"I think you've hypnotized yourself. Do you think your wife would want you to go on grieving this way?"

"I am not grieving. Not in the way you

mean. It is simply that I find neither life nor people very tolerable. There is nothing to work for." He did not know why he continued to talk to this absurd girl.

"Yet you work." She continued to prod him.

He nodded unwillingly. "I work. I work to keep from thinking."

"You need someone to be interested in."

"Who? A woman?" He looked directly at her, and again the color in her bright cheeks spread. "There never will be another woman."

"I didn't mean a woman, although I think you are boasting a little. You are still a young man, Mr. Merrill, and there are any number of attractive women in the world."

He did not answer this.

"I was thinking of someone else, of the boy Clarence Donovan, for instance. You could take him, you could perhaps make a man of him. You imagine that your life is without purpose. Create a purpose."

It was outside his experience that anyone should talk to him in this manner, least of all a perfectly strange hotel clerk, yet he found himself answering her seriously.

"I doubt that anything could be done for that sniveling little coward."

"Are you afraid to try?"

"Why should I be afraid?"

"Then do it. You are the one man in whom he believes. What do you have to lose?"

His answer surprised him, and he was still surprised when he found himself having dinner that night with Clarence Donovan and Mary Campbell in the corner of the hotel kitchen.

The boy was ill at ease, uncertain, and he would have been suspicious had the girl not been present, for in the few hours since they had met he had developed an adoration toward her that he had never given to anyone else. He had hardly spoken during the meal. He hardly took his eyes from her, and it was with a distinct sense of loss that he saw her push back her chair and rise.

"You will excuse me, please. It is past my time for bed."

She was gone then, leaving the man and the boy gripped for a moment in a mutually embarrassed silence.

Then Merrill found a cigar, put it between his lips, and lit it, examining the boy through the resulting smoke.

"How much education do you have? Can you read and write?"

The boy bobbed his head dumbly.

"How are you in arithmetic?"

For the first time since their meeting

Clarence Donovan smiled. "I like it."

Merrill's voice was cold, and the smile went away from the boy's lips. "I didn't ask that. I asked how good you are."

"Well, I did all the sums they gave me."

"Multiplication?"

Merrill got a nod for answer.

"Long division?"

Again the nod.

"I don't suppose you know what algebra, geometry, or trigonometry are?"

"I don't."

"You'll learn. That is, if you want to."

"Learn?"

"Yes, learn. I'm going to make an engineer out of you if I can. It's up to you. It isn't going to be easy. You probably didn't get through high school."

"I had one year. . . ."

"All right, you'll have to make up the rest."

Clarence Donovan considered this in numbed silence. Finally he said, "Who's going to teach me?"

"I am."

Again the silence, and at last he asked in a small voice, "Why are you doing this for me?"

Gordon Merrill pondered slowly. Why was he doing it? Certainly not for the boy. There was not one appealing quality about him.

For Mary Campbell? Why should he do anything for her? Another pretty girl who nettled him. For himself then? That, too, was absurd. What earthly good was there in saddling himself with this scared kid?

"What's the difference?" he said. "Now, ask me some questions, any questions about anything. I just want to see how your mind works."

The boy sat frozen. Merrill prompted him. "Aren't you curious about anything? How far it is to the moon, what's the name of the North Star, what makes a steam engine work?"

Clarence Donovan cleared his throat. "Well . . . I always wondered how gold got mixed up with all that sand they're washing out of the mountain over at the pit. . . ."

"Good for you." Merrill felt an actual lift of interest. If the kid had wondered about where gold came from and why, it was at least a beginning, a place to start.

"I'm not going to try to give you a geology lesson, not yet. But, when the earth was formed it was a molten mass, red-hot, like the sun."

"What held it together?"

"Never mind that for the moment. All matter is found in one of three states, depending on its temperature: liquid, like water, gas, and solid. . . . You've seen ice."

"Yes."

"And steam?"

"Yes." There was a rising excitement in the boy's tone as if he were beginning to play a game that he enjoyed.

"All right. Ice, water, and steam are all the same thing. Their chemical formula is $H_2O$. That means that water is a combination of two parts of hydrogen and one part of oxygen."

The boy's bewildered look warned Merrill that it was going too fast.

"Don't try to understand that part just yet. The point here is that like any other element, gold can be melted by heat to a liquid form and, if the heat is sufficient, to gas.

"Now, when the earth began to cool, a hard crust was formed on its outside. From time to time the heat and gas caught inside tried to push out, forming cracks and chimneys, filling them with a liquid combination of metals and rocks. You know what a volcano is?"

The boy's eyes lighted. Merrill noted the spark and went on.

"Not all the cracks were as big as volcanos. Some were merely rips in the crust, and these filled with a liquid that hardened as it cooled into a rock we call quartz. You've seen quartz?"

Anyone who had been around a gold mining region for any length of time knew quartz, and the boy grinned. Merrill nodded.

"This quartz that filled the cracks in the crust we call veins. It cooled and hardened, and then the gas pressure inside fractured it, cracked it, and liquid gold forced up into those fissures. That's what makes our lode mines."

"But the sand . . . how did the gold get into that?"

"I'm coming to that. At one time the two big valleys at the foot of these hills was a sea of water, and the big rivers ran north and south instead of east and west as they now do. They were called tertiary streams because they flowed during the tertiary geologic period. In those ancient times the running water cut down through the quartz veins and broke loose the tiny particles of gold caught in them. The gold was heavy and settled to the bottom of those stream beds.

"That mountain they are washing away at the pit was once the bed of one of those old streams. The sand that holds the gold was the sand of the river bed."

Clarence Donovan thought this over, nodding as if to himself. "Then it's kind of like the placer mines down on the mother lode."

"Yes," said Merrill. "But the modern rivers of the mother lode collected the gold from the old tertiary river beds as the new rivers cut their canyons across the old. Now, that's enough for one night. Where do you sleep?"

The boy shrugged. "Well, I was sleeping in the bunkhouse, but since I ran out on Harmony . . ."

"I'll see Park Campbell and get you a room."

Merrill rose and went out into the lobby, finding the hotel man behind the desk reading a week-old San Francisco newspaper. The boy followed him hesitantly, took the key Merrill handed him, and climbed the stairs. The hotel man glanced after him and chuckled.

"I see my niece is taking over another cripple."

Merrill turned to look at him, saying dryly, "I'd rather say that she shoved him into my lap."

Campbell laughed easily. He reached under the desk, brought out a square black bottle and two glasses, and poured each a third full.

"She's that way," he said casually. "I guess all women are."

Campbell's personal history was familiar to Merrill. It was known from one end of the lode to the other, for the ex-professor never made any secret of it when he was drinking.

"You sound as if you don't like women."

Campbell's laugh was full-bodied. "My dear Merrill, there probably never was a man who walked the earth who loved the ladies more. But loving them and living with them are two quite different propositions.

"I might have married Sarah, whom I adored, and in the end I would have come to hate her, and something that was fine, was glorious, would have been lost. I prefer my memory."

He drained his glass and refilled it, making a motion toward Merrill's, who refused with a shake of his head.

"That's rather a barbaric view."

"To the contrary," Campbell assured him. "It's the only civilized way a thinking man can approach a mawkish situation. You meet a woman, you are physically attracted to her. There is nothing wrong in that. We are all fundamentally animal in our reactions. But because she appeals to us for the moment we are asked to accept her as a permanent yoke around our necks. For make no mistake, Mr. Merrill, although women are in a sense second-class citizens, it is the women who rule our society, insidiously, through their power over men."

Merrill looked closely at Campbell, wondering just how drunk the older man was.

"I can't see where your application holds out here. The west, for the last fifteen years, has been a male society. How many women are there in Dayton?"

"You mean good women?"

Merrill made a face, then used a short, scornful laugh. "I suppose I do."

"Twelve. And we have nearly a thousand men working in the pit. But may I tell you something, Mr. Merrill; aside from my niece, those twelve women are married to the business leaders of the camp, and if you don't think their word is law to their men you know very little about women."

Maybe I don't, thought Merrill, but Ellen wasn't like that. Ellen . . . he had not actually stopped to think about her for a long time. He had consciously not thought about her. But now he was remembering something. It had been his wife who had insisted on accompanying him underground on that fateful day. He had not wanted her to go because he had feared the timbering. Yet he had not argued. He realized now that he had seldom argued with her during their year of marriage.

"I guess I don't," he said aloud.

Park Campbell poured another drink into Merrill's glass, and Gordon drank it automatically.

"I don't disparage women," Campbell went on. "I honor them. In a way I worship them. It is because of this that I never married. A goddess is destroyed by too much familiarity. I would rather live with my dreams."

Gordon Merrill felt the heat of the liquor run down through him. He had always drunk sparingly, having little patience with those who addled their brains with alcohol, and he was definitely feeling the whiskey now. He found himself liking this spare little man as he had liked few people in the last years. Maybe it was the alcohol. Maybe he should try getting drunk. But he had seen too many men try to wipe out their troubles that way. It had never worked for them and he knew that it would not work for him.

Park Campbell was saying, "Women are tougher than men. What man could actually look forward toward labor, toward the pain of childbirth? And who but a woman would climb out of a sickbed in Massachusetts and drag herself across the plains in an effort to save her life when the doctors had given up hope?"

"Who was that?" said Merrill.

"My niece. Didn't you know? She has consumption."

# CHAPTER FIVE

Austin Cleaver had had four drinks from the square bottle on the scarred table by the time the door opened and George Spain came into the saloon's rear room. Spain was a big man, standing an even six feet, with heavy shoulders and powerful arms and hands, a handsome man aside from the tight, cruel line of his mouth and his stone-gray eyes.

He shut the door, using his heel, and moved over to the table, sinking onto its top. The coat he wore was sheep-lined and made him look even larger.

Cleaver looked at him. "Merrill got here."

"A day early."

"Yeah."

"What happened?"

"He fired me."

Spain sat very still. "I've been planning for three years to kill him. I missed because he went out of the country. I'll take care of him tonight."

"No."

"What do you mean, no?" The big man reached out, ignoring the glass, taking up the bottle and drinking directly from its neck. "You or nobody else is going to keep me from killing Gordon Merrill."

"I have no intention of trying to keep you from it. The day you do I'll dance happily on his grave, but I don't want him killed yet."

"Why not?"

"Because if Merrill is dead Trueblood and the damned directors will send another man down to find out what happened to their gold."

"And if he isn't killed he'll find out."

"Not if we get hold of him. Not if we send reports in his name that he's looking into things but that he wants to move cautiously. All we need is thirty days' time. Bromley is quietly buying up stock and rounding up options. If we can hold out until the day the new board is elected, we're in control of Magnus. Then who is going to ask any questions about any missing gold?"

Spain thought this over in silence. "Couldn't we just knock him on the head and send the reports as if he were still alive?"

"We can't. Someone would tell San Francisco that he's missing. He's got to be around the pit where people can see him. The idea will be to keep him in the office, and let only men whom we can trust within speaking distance of him."

"That's not going to be easy to do."

"No," said Austin Cleaver. "Very little that is worth doing in this world is easy, but we can manage. Get three or four men, wait until everyone at the hotel has turned in for the night. Take him over to the office and put him in the bunk room at the rear."

George Spain did not like the idea, but he could think of no better one. George Spain was not given to much thinking. He had always prided himself on being a man of action.

He left the saloon, not aware that the old swamper watched him with curious eyes and after a momentary hesitation followed him into the dark out of doors. The only illumination came from the lamps set in the store and bar windows. Spain's big figure moved through one patch of light and then another until he reached a small saloon at the lower end of the street. He disappeared inside, to return a few minutes later accompanied by three other men.

The four of them came silently back up the street, past the Pit, and on toward the hotel, turning wordlessly in through the door.

A lamp still burned in the lobby but there was no one behind the desk and there was no sound from the kitchen. Spain catfooted to the desk, reversed the register, and looked at the room number opposite Gordon Merrill's name, then he turned toward the stairs, motioned his men to follow him.

They climbed, their weight making the old boards creak, and continued along the hall to the rear. Gordon Merrill's door was not locked. Merrill had never in his life locked a door.

He heard the door open, and his hand moved to the gun beneath his pillow, but he was not fast enough, for Spain was through the door and on him like a well-muscled cat, wrapping the covers around him in a cocoon, pinioning his arms, muttering, "Shut the door. Make a light."

Behind him a match flared, and one of the men lifted the lamp's chimney. Gordon found himself staring up into George Spain's heavy face, and his first thought was that death had at last sought him out.

He had not known that Spain was in Dayton, although he should have guessed it, for the Spain brothers had been with Austin Cleaver at both White Pine and

Virginia City.

For eight years he had wondered how it would be to die. He had been certain that he did not care, and he had never really understood why he did not turn his gun upon himself. But he had never before been faced with what seemed certain death.

He knew George Spain. The man was a killer by instinct. The only human lives he valued were his own and that of his brother Tom, and it was impossible that he would forget or forgive the man who had shot Tom down.

So it was with deep surprise that Merrill felt Spain reach beneath the pillow, get the gun, and then step back, with greater surprise that he heard him say, "All right, Gordon. Get dressed."

Gordon Merrill threw back the covers and swung his feet to the floor. His clothes lay on the chair at the bedside, and he dressed, not hurriedly yet neither purposely dragging out the operation. Finally he straightened.

Spain said, "We're going to walk out of here and over to the pit. If you want to live don't speak to anyone, and don't try to get away. The odds aren't on your side."

He nodded to his men to open the door, then Merrill was shepherded out, along the hall and down the stairs and across the lobby without seeing anyone but his four captors.

In the darkness of the doorway across from the hotel Jason Comstock, the swamper, pulled back as far as he could into the concealing shadow as he saw them emerge and frowned as he recognized the white-haired man in the light from the lobby lamp. There was little in life for him save curiosity and his burning dislike of Austin Cleaver, who had fired him from the mill. He followed them down the street at a safe distance, and long before they reached the gaping gash in the mountainside which was the pit, he had guessed where they were going.

The incessant roar of the monitors was stronger here where they dashed their jets of water against the crumbling sand, under-cutting it, letting the bulk of the material above cave down of its own weight, washing the resulting piles of sand into the enormous sluice.

The group passed the mill where the jigs treated the concentrates from the sluice, separating the gold from the heavy black sand and sending it on across the copper plates whose surfaces gleamed with mer-cury.

The mine office was a substantial, single-storied building beyond the mill. It held the desks of the shift superintendents, the strong room where the gold bars were stored, and emergency sleeping quarters. It was into the rear of these quarters that Spain shoved his prisoner and motioned him to a seat on the bed.

"Cleaver will be here in a minute."

Merrill was beginning to understand. He smiled sourly. "It won't work, George. I fired him and I'm not going to take him back. You can blow the top off my head if you want to, but Austin stays fired, and if I can get any evidence of his thieving he's going to prison."

Spain sat down on a chair in the corner, glancing at his men who filled the doorway.

"You boys wait outside."

They turned and filed out, closing the door behind them. Spain grinned at Merrill. He was beginning to enjoy this. It was like a cat playing with a mouse. It would never have occurred to him to torture his victim, but he found that it was more fun than actually killing him. He would kill him in the end, but not until Merrill had served their purpose.

"Surprised that you're alive?"

Merrill said nothing. You had to shout to

be heard against the curtain of noise from the pit, and he did not feel like shouting. The door opened and Austin Cleaver came in.

He smiled at Merrill, a smile that held far more of mockery than humor, then he nodded at Spain.

"Go on out with the boys."

The man in the chair made no move to obey. He said easily, "I like it here. It's fun watching the Ghost crawl."

A trace of annoyance showed in Austin Cleaver's eyes. He was not used to having his orders questioned. But he needed George Spain yet awhile and so crowded down the feeling, turning to Merrill, walking close to him to be more easily heard.

"You're going to help us, Gordon. That is, if you hope to come out of this alive. I'd kill you tonight, but that would defeat my purpose. The men in San Francisco would merely send someone else."

Merrill said in a level tone, "This won't get you anywhere. Sooner or later they're going to catch up with you. How much have you stolen?"

Cleaver's smile widened. "Nearly five million."

Merrill had to force himself to keep from showing his astonishment. He had had no idea that the depredations ran so high. Five million in a little less than three years.

"Now I know you won't get away with it."

Cleaver's assurance was complete. "Yes we will. The thing that you don't realize, that no one realizes, is that we have used the gold to buy up stock in the Magnus Company. There is a general meeting next month to elect a new board of directors. We have the stock to elect our own board. Once we have done that we are perfectly safe. We certainly aren't going to prosecute ourselves. And, my dear half brother, we have you."

# CHAPTER SIX

Gordon Merrill stood at the window of the small room behind the mine office and looked out across the semicircle of the Dayton Pit.

Larger than the Roman Colosseum, this was a manmade amphitheater torn into the side of the mountain by the force of water.

In the light of the burning pitch fires that illumined the scene as if it were midday instead of midnight he had a panoramic view of the whole operation. It was the finest on the mother lode, and Gordon Merrill could justifiably have taken pride, for he had conceived it, designed it, and begun the work.

The pit was a consolidation of four earlier workings which had failed because of inadequate water supply and improper drainage, and when Magnus had first decided to go into hydraulic mining it had dispatched Merrill to Nevada County to look over the possibilities.

His recommendations had been basic. Buy the four small outfits, combine their systems of water ditches to connect with a new dam and reservoir to be built on the upper reaches of the Yuba. Drop a hundred-foot-deep shaft into the earth at the mountain's base, intercepting an eight-thousand-foot-long bedrock tunnel leading to the canyon of the Yuba River on the other side of the mountain range.

This all had been done. It had cost three million dollars to buy the property, construct the dam, revise the water system, and drive the tunnel. In itself the tunnel would not have been a possibility except for the new steel drills and the equally new combining of blasting powders into dynamite.

Eight thousand men had labored on the dam, the ditches, and the tunnel. Steam engines turned the creaking hurdy-gurdy wheels, driving their mechanical drills deep into the native rock at the Yuba Valley end of the tunnel. But at the shaft connection there was no room for these, and miners swung their slower single jacks. It took over a year to complete the preparations and set the mine functioning.

Now, every twenty-four hours a million feet of water flowed through the ditches into the pressure boxes high on the adjoining ridge. From the boxes iron pipes manufactured on the spot, measuring two feet in diameter at the head and decreasing as they dropped downward, squeezed the plunging stream into the huge monitor where it sat four hundred feet from the face of the cliff.

The monitor's nozzle was one of the new Hoskins Little Giants, patterned after the artillery of the Civil War, an iron cannon with a ten-inch bore. Fitted with controls so that two men could swing it easily, it brayed a constant jet, five thousand inches of water under a five-hundred-foot pressure, force enough to tear down the most solid building ever built in the country.

The mining procedure was dramatic in its simplicity. The blasting stream was directed at the base of the huge cliff-like face of sand that rose a full four hundred feet above the solid bedrock. The pounding water undercut the sand until that left hanging unsupported tumbled in a mighty avalanche.

Then the monitor flushed the fallen sand and smaller gravel into the shaft's mouth, dropping it a further hundred feet into the tunnel below, while the larger boulders and debris were dragged to one side and piled out of the way.

The shaft was built in two compartments.

Down one, mud and water swept in a never-ending cascade, down the other ran a ladder by which men could descend to the drainage tunnel.

Along the center of the tunnel floor ran a four-foot-wide, stone-lined ditch ribbed with railroad rails set as baffles every six feet. Beside the ditch a raised catwalk of wooden planks accommodated the crews.

The fines and slickens washing across the baffles dropped the heavier gold particles behind the rails, so that it was in effect a giant sluice box, eight thousand feet long.

At the terminal, the Yuba Canyon end, the tailings spewed from the tunnel's mouth, falling again, two hundred feet to the Yuba, and were carried thence by its angry waters down its tortuous course until all spilled into the great American River in the valley miles below.

As Merrill had conceived it the giant mine was geared to handle the largest possible amount of gravel with the smallest possible crew. Only two hundred men were needed to service the dam and ditches, to muck the big boulders and trees out of the way, and to supervise the tunnel.

The gravel from the mountain ran better than fifty cents a yard. Once each month the monitor halted its decimation of the cliff, and fresh, unmuddied water was poured down the shaft, rinsing the remaining traces of mud and sand from the ditch. Then the cleanup crew worked along the catwalk, raising the baffles and sweeping up the gold which had lodged behind them, dumping it into buckets containing mercury and hoisting it aloft to be treated later.

When Gordon Merrill first opened the operation engineers from all over the mountains came to see it work, and the value of Magnus Mining soared on the San Francisco stock exchange. But the company had not returned a dividend for a full year now, and Merrill knew that more gold had been stolen from the mine than had been delivered to the company's strong room. The thought brought a deep, smoldering anger to him. It was not that he owned stock in the company. It was not that he felt sorry for Boris Trueblood and his associates. It was rather that in the final sense he was a company man.

Magnus Mining had been his life. He had sweated and frozen, thirsted and starved for it in the four corners of the world. It was the only life he had, the only solid thing he could tie to. And Austin Cleaver, who owed as much to Boris Trueblood as Merrill did, had betrayed the trust, had nearly wrecked the company that Gordon Merrill had worked so hard to help build.

Merrill turned away from the window and sat down on the end of the narrow, hard bunk. He had no fear for himself. He did not care whether or not he lived, but he did not want to die until he settled with Austin Cleaver and George Spain.

The question was how best to proceed. He could refuse to take their orders. He could refuse to leave the office, to be seen around the pit by the workmen. If Trueblood did not hear from him within a few days he would send someone else from San Francisco to investigate. But whoever was sent would probably fall into the same trap he had, and Cleaver and Spain were playing for high stakes, for control of one of the greatest mining empires in history.

Another man would have stayed awake that night, but Gordon Merrill had long since schooled himself to take his rest when he could, never knowing what the next day would bring. He hauled off his boots and pants, and, still wearing his heavy shirt, he blew out the lamp and crawled beneath the thin blankets.

Morning came to Dayton, a thin streak in the east, a gray light silhouetting the tall pines which towered along the ridges like sentinels guarding the precious valley.

Harmony Jones was the first man in the bunkhouse to wake. He rose and scratched, stepping out to the wash bench beyond the back door. He shivered in the early chill as he dipped water into the granite pan and washed noisily. Then he went back inside to stoke up the big range, cursing Clarence Donovan with a comfortable anger. He would skin the kid's backside when the boy showed up, for the big cook never doubted that the runaway would reappear as soon as hunger growled loudly enough in his flattish stomach.

Mary Campbell was awake. She had slept lightly through the night, troubled by something which she did not quite understand. Perhaps it was the boy or perhaps the gray-haired man, for she found both their presences unsettling in her ordered existence.

She rose and, wearing a heavy robe, moved into the kitchen for warm water from the tank in the stove. Her bedroom was on the ground floor because her uncle had not felt that the exertion of climbing the stairs was good for her.

Hop Lee, the cook, was already stirring the banked fire. He glanced at her, his yellow face and button eyes showing no expression. She often wondered what went on in the small head beneath the carefully wrapped pigtail, for she was certain that Hop Lee was her friend. But his supply of English was limited and her knowledge of pidgin too sketchy to allow of much communication between them.

There was a noise at the door behind her, and she turned to see Clarence Donovan come hesitantly into the room, and she smiled.

"Good morning."

She saw the flush of embarrassment on his thin face and realized that it bothered him, her wearing a robe and not being fully dressed.

"It's all right," she said, trying to put him at his ease. "I have not been well. I spend at least a part of each day in bed."

Quick concern came into his eyes, and he muttered, "I didn't know. . . . I . . ."

"And stop apologizing. That's the first thing you have to learn. Now you can help by setting the table for breakfast."

He took the plates and the cutlery, carrying them into the long dining room. She got her pan of hot water and retreated to her bedroom, going directly to the small round iron stove. She lit the kindling it contained and felt the welcome heat begin to radiate.

Breakfast at the hotel was not an ordered meal. The guests appeared by ones and twos, giving their order to Sadie Thorne, the waitress. Sadie was thirty-five. She weighed nearly two hundred pounds and was married to one of the monitor men at the Dayton pit. A big, cheerful woman without a brain in her head; that was the way Park Campbell had described her to his niece when Mary had first arrived, and the girl had learned to agree. Sadie was a good worker but she talked incessantly. Mary could hear the rattle of her chatter through the kitchen door as she finished dressing and started for the dining room.

The fact that Cleaver was at the table made her think of Gordon Merrill, and she wondered what was keeping the mining engineer. After what he had said about Austin Cleaver the preceding evening she was curious to see them together. She pushed open the connecting door and, moving along the table, took her place at the end.

Austin Cleaver jumped to his feet to pull the chair out for her, to smile and say, "Good morning."

She nodded. "Good morning."

"You never looked nicer."

She felt herself flush. Austin Cleaver was a handsome man, and his self-assurance had roused her curiosity from the first. She looked at him quickly, expecting him to show some nervousness because of Merrill's presence in town, but he seemed entirely unconcerned.

She ate slowly, listening to the spate of talk around the board. Aside from Sadie, who was constantly on the move between the kitchen and dining room, she was the only woman. There were three salesmen, Cleaver, Spain, and four merchants who, being bachelors, lived at the hotel.

She considered them, speculating. By all odds Cleaver was the most attractive. He was younger than the rest, and his speech showed his background and education.

She finished and rose in silence, returning to the kitchen to find Clarence Donovan eating at the kitchen table.

"You don't have to eat out here."

His color rose again, and she could feel his unease. "I like it here."

"Clarence," she said, "you can't hide from the world for the rest of your life. You've got to face things, like Mr. Merrill does."

He did not move. His expression did not change.

"Speaking of Mr. Merrill" — she changed the subject — "he must have overslept. We don't serve breakfast after eight-thirty.

Would you go up and tell him?"

The boy bobbed his head, rose hastily, and headed for the dining room, but she said, "It's quicker to use the back stairs."

When he had gone she sat down at the table, writing out the menus for the noon meal in her careful, rounded script. She heard his heavy shoes come back down the hollow stairs like a bat dragged across a picket fence, then he burst into the kitchen, his face open with agitation.

"He ain't there."

She started to correct his grammar, then stopped, not wanting to make him more conscious of his linguistic deficiencies than he already was.

"So?"

"And his stuff is gone."

"Who's gone?" Park Campbell had just come in from the dining room.

"Mr. Merrill."

"Even his stuff's gone." It was the boy.

The hotel man shrugged. "Doesn't make much sense. Ghost Merrill isn't the kind to run out without paying his hotel bill."

"Of course he didn't. That's absurd." Mary Campbell spoke with more vehemence than she intended. "Something must have happened to him."

Her uncle glanced at her with sharpened

attention. Park Campbell had lived for a long time, and he had spent most of it studying the people around him. He said dryly, "Nothing much happens to Ghost Merrill that he doesn't want to happen. I wouldn't worry."

He stood for a long minute, smiling at her his half secretive smile, then he turned away, back through the dining room and lobby and entered the barroom at the other side of the building.

There was no one in the dimly lit room, yet it had the feel of occupancy in the warm residue of tobacco smoke that pervaded the walls. He rounded the bar, found his private bottle in its hiding place, and poured himself his first drink of the day.

Standing there at the worn counter, the small glass cupped in his hand, he considered life and sighed. He was very fond of his niece. She was the only member of his rather large family who had showed him any tolerance, and he needed the feeling of not being alone, of actually belonging to someone.

"I hope she doesn't get herself mixed up with him."

The words were muttered aloud to the empty room. The "him" he referred to was Gordon Merrill. There was something about the white-haired man that troubled Park Campbell. He poured the liquor down his throat, rinsed the glass, returned it to its place, and went back to the kitchen in search of breakfast.

Clarence took no notice. He stepped out onto the street, wondering where to start, for he had decided to find Merrill. He walked without direction, down Dayton's main thoroughfare, trying to make up his mind. The only one in camp whom he could think of who knew Merrill was Harmony Jones, and he had no intention of getting anywhere near the fat cook if he could help it.

Suddenly he thought of the livery stable. If Gordon Merrill had ridden out of camp the liveryman would know. He turned, retracing his steps past the hotel. It was still so early that there were few people on the sidewalk and almost no one in the stores. He reached the stable's corral and ducked through it to the barn at the rear.

The hostler was swamping out the stalls, a short man with stocky shoulders, a broad, flat face, and thin gray hair. He looked up, nodding as Clarence came in.

"Hello, kid. Harmony was around the saloons looking for you last night."

A finger of fear ran through Clarence.

"You didn't tell him where I was?"

"I didn't know," said Paddy Karger, "but I'll tell him when I see him."

"Don't." Panic made the thin voice quaver. "He'll skin me alive."

"For what?"

"For running away when he needed help."

Paddy Karger jabbed his fork into the manure at his feet and leaned on the oak handle. "It's a free country, boy. You don't belong to that gut bucket of a cook. You don't belong to no one but yourself."

"Sure," said Clarence Donovan, and the defensive sneer which had almost disappeared from his voice in the last few hours was back. "It's easy for you to say, if you never had a man take a strap to you."

Paddy grinned. "The last man who tried was my old pa, and I broke his crown before I ran away. If it's a horse you're wanting . . ."

"I'm looking for Gordon Merrill. You know him?"

Paddy Karger showed his surprise. "The Ghost? Who doesn't know him?"

"He's gone from the hotel. I thought maybe you saw him ride out."

The hostler shook his head. "That's his horse, the bay in the end stall. He ain't been here since I come to work at midnight."

The boy turned away. The man looked after him curiously. "And what would you be wanting with Merrill?"

"He's a friend of mine." Clarence Donovan hitched his faded trousers. "A very good friend. I've got a message for him."

# CHAPTER SEVEN

The mine pit had always drawn Clarence Donovan. He had hung around it every spare moment since he had reached camp. The roar of the huge jet of water had been frightening at first. The destructive force of that stream was nearly past his imagination. He stood now, watching as the two operators turned the giant monitor in its slow arc, watching as the water struck the base of the cut, watching the sand and small boulders fly a hundred feet in the air.

The flowing probe ate steadily, back and forth, back and forth, undercutting the bank, gnawing a trench in the face thirty feet high. As Clarence stood, the cut deepened until suddenly there was a rumbling, gathering roar loud enough to be heard above the constant howl of the monitor, and the whole face collapsed in a landslide which carried thousands of tons of rock and sand crashing into a great pile at the foot of the cliff. Trees fifty feet high which a moment before had been standing on the top of the mountain far above, looking as indestructible as monuments, tumbled down the slope, their branches splintering like matchsticks, the main trunk shattering like dried oat stems under the impact of the rolling, falling rocks.

Clarence shuddered as he did with each cave-out. The appalling forces of nature that men had harnessed to do their handiwork both fascinated and repelled him. He turned away as the monitor men swung their water stream against the freshly fallen rubble, washing it methodically toward the shaft head. He moved toward the mine office, meaning to ask whoever was there if he had seen Merrill, but before he could reach the door Jean Armand stepped from the doorway.

Armand was a slight, very dark French Canadian. About forty, he still moved with a quick controlled step, and there was no person more feared in Dayton. Head of the mine police, he had killed three men since Clarence had come to camp, and the boy was deadly afraid of him. He blocked the entrance, unsmiling.

"Where do you think you're going, kid?"

Clarence stopped. He hunted words. His

tongue felt too thick for the cavity of his mouth. He tried three times to speak before he managed to say, "I'm looking for Gordon Merrill."

As he spoke he raised his eyes beyond the guard and saw Merrill watching him through the office window. The knowledge that Merrill was there bolstered his courage.

"There he is now."

He raised his hand to greet the man at the window. Gordon Merrill did not move. He made no indication that he even recognized the boy. He stood for a moment where he was, then turned away.

Armand said, "Merrill's busy. He don't want to be bothered." His voice had the slurring rapidity of his native language, yet he spoke with hardly a trace of accent.

Clarence Donovan stared at him, a surprising anger rising within him. Then he said with more heat than he intended, "Just tell him that Mary Campbell was worried about him. He might have had the decency to let her know he was leaving the hotel."

He spoke loudly. Anyone around the pit automatically raised his voice to compete with the monitors, so that the anger in his tone hardly reached Armand. The boy made an about-face and marched back across the rough ground of the pit floor and climbed the small ridge which separated the mine from the town's main street.

Gordon Merrill watched him leave with a sense of frustration such as he seldom experienced. He took two short turns around the confining room, spinning when Armand opened the door and came in.

"What did the boy want?"

Armand shrugged. He smiled, showing badly stained teeth. Watching him, Merrill was unfavorably reminded of a weasel. Austin Cleaver could not have chosen a better jailer. Armand was as deadly as a rattlesnake, and in the five years Merrill had known him he had never shown one trace of human compassion. At the moment he was taking a savage joy in lording it over a man of whom he had been jealous for a long time.

Gordon Merrill had driven him out of Bodie, and the memory still rankled. He and Merrill had run into each other head on, but it had been Armand who backed away, Armand who saddled a horse and rode out in the middle of the night after boasting that he would eat Merrill for breakfast. It was a corrosive memory the French Canadian could neither forgive nor forget. It was a stain upon his reputation, and it ate at him with the annoying finality of a creeping cancer. That there existed someone from whom he had once run he found difficult to live with.

He stood watching the younger man with maliciously mocking eyes, not speaking until Gordon repeated, "What did the kid want?"

"That girl at the hotel. She is worried about you."

Merrill's surprise was real. "And why should Mary Campbell be worried about me?"

"Who knows?" said the Frenchman with a flutter of his hands. "One can never guess what crazy things come to a woman's mind. You smiled at her perhaps. You're said to be charming, Mr. Merrill, though I have never found you so."

"I know you haven't," Merrill told him shortly. "I should have put a bullet in you at Bodie instead of letting you sneak off like a rat in the dark."

Armand flushed deep. He drew his gun and stood balancing it in his fingers.

"You know, Merrill, I've often thought it would be very much fun to pistol whip you."

He came forward two catlike steps, stopping, watching the other's eyes as if expecting Merrill to show fear. Gordon Merrill did not move. He did not speak, but his thin lips curved slightly in a tight smile. The Frenchman took another step, then the door behind him opened and Austin Cleaver entered. He realized the situation in a glance, saying sharply, "That's enough, Jean. Get out of here."

The man hesitated, then with an expressive shrug he dropped the gun into its holster, pivoted, and left the office.

Cleaver sat down in the chair behind the scarred desk, examining Merrill as if he were a curiosity from another planet.

"You know, Gordon, for one who is rated the smartest engineer in the business you show very little common judgment. A lot of people hate you with good reason, but I doubt if there is any man in the whole mother lode country who hates you as thoroughly as Jean Armand does."

Merrill did not trouble to answer.

"So if you want to stay alive you had best watch your tongue with him. He'd as soon cut your throat and drink your blood as he would breathe."

Merrill shrugged. "You wouldn't understand, Austin, but the only reason I care to stay alive is to see that you get exactly what is coming to you."

Cleaver laughed. "For a hard-boiled character you have a curious sentimental streak.

Ten years now you've been grieving over Ellen. Fifteen years you've been pulling me out of one jack pot after another, not because you liked me but because of our tainted relationship. And now when you are finally up against a situation you can't beat the only reason you want to stay alive is to see that I am punished."

Gordon Merrill watched him, showing no indication of reaction.

"Every man," Cleaver went on, "has an Achilles' heel. I guess I'm yours. I've stood in your way all of your life. I had the name you wanted for yourself. My mother had the position and acceptance that your mother longed for."

Merrill said in a low tone, "And we had something of more importance, which neither you nor your mother ever really had. We had your father, his love and his companionship."

Austin Cleaver's face lost color until his tan looked a leaden gray. He said in a constricted voice, "It would give me real pleasure to kill you. Believe me."

"I don't doubt it," Merrill told him. "But you never will. You inherited the weakness of your mother's family. You have no strength to stand and fight. Neither had your mother. She tried to hold our father to her by weakness, by pretended illness, by all the cheating ways in which a weak woman tries to cling to a man."

Cleaver got slowly to his feet. When he spoke his tone was not steady, but he managed to say, "I know what you are trying to do now. You're trying to goad me into a fight, into killing you. But it won't work, my wily brother. I'm playing for too much. Thirty days are all I need, and I will have them no matter what it costs me."

He forced himself to turn and pull open the door, and Merrill almost admired the man's control.

Then through the doorway Merrill had a glimpse of Jean Armand and George Spain standing a dozen feet away. He saw someone else. Mary Campbell was picking her way across the rough ground toward the office.

Cleaver saw her also. He stopped in surprise, hesitated for a moment, then swung back. To Merrill he said harshly, "The girl from the hotel is outside."

"I saw her."

"She's come down to find you. I don't know why, but I heard what the boy said to Armand."

Merrill made no answer.

"So you're going outside. You're going to tell her that you moved out of the hotel because there is so much work here that you haven't time to leave the pit."

Merrill's expression was sardonic. "You think she'll believe that?"

Cleaver's voice was taut. "She'd better believe it if you don't want her hurt. I meant what I said, Gordon. No one, not even Mary Campbell, gets in our way now. If she were to suspect anything she might decide to send word to San Francisco. We'd have to stop her, and I'm not joking."

Merrill looked at his brother's eyes and found a deep mockery there. He nodded slightly to show that Cleaver had won his point, then started out through the open doorway toward the oncoming girl.

At sight of him both Jean Armand and George Spain stiffened, but Cleaver stepped into their view, making a hand signal. They stood undecided for a moment, then moved off as Gordon Merrill paused before the girl.

She stopped, putting her fists on her hips, and he saw that her eyes were dark with anger.

"You might at least have had the courtesy to tell us you were checking out."

His shrug was convincing. "I'm sorry. Actually I never thought of it. I couldn't sleep. I got to worrying about the mine and started down here. Then I remembered the room behind the office which I had used when I opened the mine, so I took my gear with me."

She looked at him levelly and there was anger in her tone. "And I believed you when you said you'd help Clarence. You wouldn't even talk to him this morning. I hope you are proud of yourself, Mr. Merrill. That boy needed you. He thought he'd found a friend. Now that you have failed him I don't know what he will do."

She finished, then marched away, her head held high. Behind Merrill, Cleaver laughed with evident relish.

"That should take care of you, Ghost. Actually I'm not too sorry this happened. She's been a little difficult to get to know. I may have better luck from now on."

Merrill spoke slowly. "Leave her alone."

"What's she to you?"

"Nothing. But at least she's a decent person, and you've harmed every woman you've touched."

"I'll think about it," said Cleaver, and went back into the building.

Merrill stared after him, then walked slowly to a straight chair which stood against the outside wall and eased himself down into it. If he could get a message through to Trueblood. How? He thought of

Clarence Donovan. If some way he could get a note to the boy, send him to Grass Valley to the telegraph line . . .

But what was the way? He saw that George Spain and Jean Armand were eying him and knew that they would watch him every minute of the day and night.

He had been tempted to alert the girl, but he did not want her in any way involved. He remembered the shock Park Campbell's words had brought him on the preceding evening, when the older man had told him that Mary had consumption.

It was hard to believe she was ill. There was a quality of aliveness about her which he had never associated with people who were ill. For himself, he had not been sick a full day of his life. He had no experience, and like a great many people, he feared what he did not understand.

And yet, sick as she undoubtedly was, this girl had walked the mile from the hotel merely to tell him what she thought of him. At first he put the action down as a kind of vindictiveness, but as he thought about it more carefully he decided that she had been motivated not so much by anger at him as by her feeling for Clarence Donovan. She had apparently adopted the boy and his troubles as her own. And she was shrewd enough to realize that Clarence needed a man he could trust, a man he could look up to.

Merrill's thin lips twisted in self-mockery. Certainly of all the men in the world she could have picked on to give the boy an example, he was the worst. He rose with a sudden wave of impatience and strode into the office.

# Chapter Eight

Mary Campbell marched up Dayton's main street in a kind of vacuum. She could not recall having ever been as angry at anyone as she was at Gordon Merrill.

It was, she realized, her own fault. On a very casual acquaintance she had drawn a mental picture of the man which was not at all in keeping with reality. Gordon Merrill was what he was, what life had made him, a cold, self-centered man nursing a grief that should have been long-buried.

And she had hoped to draw him out of himself. She wondered how much her interest was with the boy, how much with the man. For above all she was entirely honest with herself.

Jason Comstock came out through the door of the Pit saloon as she passed and stopped to remove his hat.

She smiled at him automatically, hardly seeing him. She knew his story well. Once he had been a prosperous miningman, but gambling and women and finally drink had dropped him to the bottom of the ladder, and there seemed no hope of return.

"You're out early, miss."

His words were only slightly slurred, and she judged that he was fairly sober. On impulse she said, "Come up to the hotel for breakfast."

She saw him stiffen and guessed that the remnants of his pride would not permit him to accept a favor from a woman no matter how hungry he might be. She added quickly, "There's a wagonload of wood that needs unloading, and Hop Lee doesn't have the time."

Jason Comstock relaxed at that. He replaced his hat on his unkempt hair and spoke with a courtly grace.

"If I can oblige." Without further hesitation he fell into step with her.

They walked in silence to the hotel, across the lobby, and into the kitchen. Clarence Donovan was at the sink, washing up the breakfast dishes. He turned, his pinched face questioning.

"Did you see Merrill?"

Mary Campbell's voice was short. "I saw more of him than I wanted to. He's the rudest man I've ever met."

Jason Comstock had been depositing his broken hat on the chair beside the table. He straightened.

"You talking about the Ghost? He's all right, is he?"

"All right?" The girl faced him. "And why shouldn't Mr. Gordon Merrill be all right?"

The old man shook his head. "I didn't know. There was funny things going on in town last night, and the Ghost has more enemies than most."

Her tone was waspish. "He's all right this morning, and he's running precisely true to form."

She turned away, but Clarence Donovan said, "What funny things?"

Comstock rubbed the side of his shaggy head with a calloused palm.

"Well, first Austin Cleaver comes to the saloon yesterday. He sends me to find George Spain, and he's mighty mysterious about it."

The girl, who had started for the stove, stopped. "And what's that to do with Merrill?"

"I'm coming to that. So later, I don't recollect the time, I'd had a few drinks, you understand . . ." He broke off for a moment in apology. "I saw them bring Merrill out of the hotel."

"Bring him out? Who?"

"Why, George Spain and some men. They had a gun in his back."

Mary Campbell was now staring at the old man. She had a feeling of unreality. She had been in Dayton long enough to become accustomed to a certain amount of Saturday night violence, but the idea that George Spain, who took all of his meals at the hotel, should be engaged in a kidnaping . . .

"I don't believe it. Why should George Spain do a thing like that?"

The old swamper shrugged. "He and the Ghost have tangled before, and Merrill killed Spain's brother in Virginia. Not that it wasn't self-defense, you understand."

Mary Campbell passed a slow hand across her eyes as if to clear her muddled thoughts.

"But why? . . . I talked to Merrill only a few minutes ago. He didn't say anything. He didn't seem upset."

Comstock continued to shake his head. "It ain't often you can tell whether Merrill's upset or not. As for why, I don't know. All I'm sure of is that Austin Cleaver sent me to find George Spain, and later George took Merrill from the hotel. You ask me, they're holding him a prisoner for some reason."

"But he came outdoors to talk to me."

"And was anyone standing near?"

She thought a moment before she nodded. "Yes. George Spain and Jean Armand were standing about twenty feet away."

"And was the Ghost wearing his gun?"

She thought about this. "I honestly don't know. I was too angry to pay much attention to things like that."

The old man said, "Chances are he wasn't. He didn't have it on when they took him out of the hotel, and I can't see them giving it back to him. Not them. It would be like signing their own death warrants."

"But . . . what are we going to do?"

Suddenly the years of failure swept over Jason Comstock like an engulfing tide. Once he would have known what to do. Once he would have stood up to any man in camp. But those days were far in the past. He knew himself for exactly what he was, and that knowledge brought a welling of tears to his rheumy eyes.

"There ain't nothing we can do. Cleaver runs this camp, and his mine police make short work of anyone who tries to interfere." His aged shoulders sagged, and he slumped into the seat at the scrubbed kitchen table.

The girl turned toward the door, then turned back, saying to the Chinese cook, who had been watching the proceedings without comprehension, "Give him break-

96

fast, Hop."

Again she started for the door, and Clarence Donovan followed her.

"Where are you going?"

"To talk to Merrill again. To find out what is going on."

The boy's native fear was uppermost. "You shouldn't go down there, not if Comstock is telling the truth."

"Someone has to."

"Your uncle."

She considered for a moment, then shook her head. She was very fond of Park Campbell but she had few illusions about him. He was, in the final analysis, only one step above Jason Comstock.

"No."

"Then let me go."

She looked up at him quickly, reading the fear behind his eyes, knowing how much it cost him to say those words. Impulsively her hand went up to clasp his bony shoulder.

"Thanks, Clarence, but it's better that I go. They won't rough up a woman. The Lord only knows what they might do to you."

She went out of the hotel then and up the sunny street, hearing the beat and whine of the monitor grow in volume as she approached the pit.

She was amazed at her own courage, for she had never considered that she was very brave, but unaccountably she felt no fear.

She spoke to a dozen people on the street and wondered why she did not stop any one of them and tell her story, yet she knew intuitively why she failed to do so.

She had never really thought about it before, but Dayton was indeed a company town. There was no law in Dayton save the company police. Jean Armand, as their head, was a deputy sheriff for the county, but the county seat was twenty-nine miles across the mountains and the trail between was barely passable. In the whole time since her arrival from the east she had never seen the sheriff or any of the county officials in Dayton.

It was borne in on her, the extreme remoteness in which they lived. At home help had been only minutes away, but here there was no help except that which a person found within himself.

She followed the track which led up over the lip and down the sand and broken rock to the pit's floor. She could see half a dozen men before the office and knew by the way they turned that they had seen her. But she never broke step as she moved forward, and Austin Cleaver came out of the group to meet her.

"What brings you back so soon?"

She faced him, thinking how very handsome he was. But there was a pettishness about him, a spoiled child's attitude, which told of a tight inner selfishness. She marveled that she had not noticed it before, but then, perhaps she had not wanted to see.

Of the whole camp he was by far the most presentable male, and the quick, almost careless small attentions he had paid her had been very welcome.

Loneliness had been almost as hard to fight as her illness, and she had been terribly homesick when she first arrived. The addresses of an educated man had eased her readjustment. Facing him now she found it hard to believe Jason Comstock's wild tale, and her words were hesitant as she said, "I want to talk to Gordon Merrill again."

"You did, just a few minutes ago."

"I know. I forgot something." It was a lame excuse, and her manner told plainly that she knew it.

Austin Cleaver for all his faults was not a fool, and he understood that something out of the ordinary was happening here. Also, he was tensely conscious of the high stakes for which he played and aware that one careless slip could bring his whole carefully planned structure tumbling about his feet. He said, a little more curtly than courtly, "Merrill's very busy now. He doesn't want to be disturbed."

She flushed at the note in his tone, but her native stubbornness showed in her own.

"I'll let him tell me that."

Austin Cleaver looked at her a little helplessly. His opinion of women and their capabilities was not high, and he had used a number of them rather roughly during his life. But he had never met one whom he found more appealing than this Mary Campbell.

Part of her appeal lay in the fact that she had fended off his casual advances neatly without giving the impression that she disliked him. And he knew that if he now refused to allow her to see Merrill he would forfeit any chance he had with her.

"Wait here," he said, and turned back toward the group about the doorway.

He said something to them that the girl could not hear, and they scattered across the pit, only Jean Armand and George Spain remaining. She watched the two sharply, knowing that she had their full attention, and saw the smirk on Jean Armand's dark face. Then Austin Cleaver reappeared and moved out to her side.

"I'm sorry." He made a helpless gesture with his hands. "I told Gordon but he said that he was too busy." He smiled. "You have to understand Gordon. He does not mean to be rude, but he has small use for women."

"You're lying." The words came out of her before she thought. Then she turned quickly away, but his hand came out to grasp her arm.

"What do you mean by that?"

She tried to pull free but his fingers were too strong.

"Let me go."

"Answer my question."

"All right," she said. "I will. George Spain and some men kidnaped Mr. Merrill from the hotel last night. Don't bother to deny it, there was a witness. I want to know what is going on."

He gaped at her.

"You don't explain it?"

"You talked to Gordon this morning."

"I did, and I thought there was something strange in his manner then, but that was before I heard about the kidnaping."

His fingers tightened. "Who saw them? That boy who was down here?"

"No."

"It was." He turned his head and motioned to Jean Armand.

The head of the mine police moved toward them, followed by George Spain. Austin Cleaver said tightly, "That kid down here this morning, the one working for Harmony at the bunkhouse, saw George and the boys take Merrill from the hotel last night."

Jean Armand looked back at Spain. The latter shrugged.

"It was dark on the street. He could have been in any of the store doorways."

Cleaver said, "Find him and bring him down here."

Mary Campbell gasped. "He had nothing to do with it. It wasn't he who told me. It was someone else."

"Who?"

"I'm not going to tell you."

"Bring the kid in."

"Please, Austin. That boy is frightened enough as it is."

"He should have kept his nose out of other people's business. Maybe he'll learn not to talk out of turn."

"But I tell you it wasn't Clarence."

"Go get him. We'll see."

Armand moved away. Spain said to Cleaver, "What are you going to do about her?"

This was the question disturbing Cleaver

at the moment.

"Put her in the office with my brother." He swung the girl around, his quick eyes running over her slender body. "I guess she hasn't got a gun hidden."

Spain grinned. "You want me to make sure?"

Cleaver said, "If I wanted anyone to make sure I'd do it myself."

Mary's face turned a dull crimson. She had been about to protest, but the protest died in her embarrassment, for she realized that neither of these men would hesitate to strip her if they thought she had a weapon concealed about her person.

Without a word she started for the office. If they were going to hold her at least she'd walk into her prison without help. She was conscious that Cleaver followed but did not turn or hesitate. When she reached the door she pushed it open and went inside. Cleaver followed her.

Gordon Merrill had been standing before the mine's flow sheet tacked to the office wall. He turned his head and his eyes flickered with surprise, then shifted to Cleaver, asking a mute question.

Cleaver laughed. "I brought you a playmate. Make her feel at home."

He backed out, pulling the door shut

behind him, leaving the girl and Merrill to stare at each other in silence. Merrill broke it first.

"What's happened now?"

She said, "Maybe you should tell me. I came down here asking to talk to you, and now I find myself a prisoner. What is Austin Cleaver trying to do?"

He said without humor, "He's stealing the Magnus Mining Company."

"Stealing it? You mean he's stealing from it?"

"He's doing both," Merrill said. "Sit down. You're liable to be here for some time." He pulled the chair away from the desk and pushed it toward her.

She settled herself, watching him, puzzlement filling her eyes.

"I don't understand."

He grinned wryly. "Like most master plans, it's not very complicated. And the funny thing about it is that he'll probably get away with it. He has stolen gold belonging to the company and used that gold to buy up the company stock. He's bought so much that he nearly has working control."

She thought about this in silence for several minutes. Finally she said, "In effect he is actually stealing from himself."

"Not quite. This is a rather long story, and

if you're to understand I'll have to give you a bit of family history."

She looked up sharply, remembering a phrase she had heard outside.

"Austin told Spain to put me in the office with his brother. Are you and Austin brothers?"

"Half brothers," Merrill told her, and his mouth twisted. "My father was Baron Cleaver. Probably that doesn't mean anything to you, but it would mean a great deal to anyone who has been in California for a long time. The gold rush produced a number of fairly wild and colorful characters, but none of them was any wilder than my father. He made and lost a dozen fortunes. He was a big man physically, and I've heard him boast that in the early days there wasn't a man from Hangtown to Sonora who could outdrink or outfight him. He helped finance the California Bank. He helped build the Pacific Railroad. He was in Virginia City before Fair and Flood and MacKay. And he started the Magnus Mining Company. . . ."

"But, I . . ."

"Let me finish, please. My father came from New York. He shipped out here with Stevenson's regiment for the Mexican War. By the time they arrived on the coast the war was over, but gold had been discovered, so he, along with a lot of his fellows, took off for the mines.

"He was successful from the first, and he sent for his wife to come west. She joined him in Marysville, and they moved to San Francisco. That was where he met my mother."

Mary Campbell had been watching him intently, noting the tautness about his mouth, the shadow behind his eyes.

"The wife wouldn't give him a divorce." The tautness had gone into his voice now. "He set her up in a house down the Peninsula. I remember as a small boy the letters she wrote him, wheedling, whining letters. She was always ill, always dying. Until the day he passed away she used illness as a hook to draw him back. And after he died she made a startling recovery. She's still alive, still in San Francisco, still playing the great lady, still Mrs. Baron Cleaver."

Watching him, Mary Campbell felt the pulse of the deep bitterness in the man, the hard, unyielding resentment against a woman she did not know.

"And she is Austin's mother?"

He nodded.

"And you and Austin hate each other."

Again he nodded. "But that part isn't important, except to explain Austin's attitude, the real reason behind his actions. You see, Magnus Mining Company was my father's last great venture. He merged or bought a dozen smaller companies and put them into one corporation. Then, being a gambler, he became overextended in the stock market. He lost control of Magnus and shot himself."

She caught her breath.

"Austin has always blamed my mother and me for his death."

"Why?"

"He said once that my mother spent too much money." Merrill laughed shortly. "She gave her life to my father. She mothered him, and babied him, and helped him when he needed help. And she died one month after he did. She simply did not want to live with him gone."

The girl was silent, remote, trying to picture this other woman who had lived with and loved a man who could not marry her.

Gordon Merrill laughed again, shortly, sharply, as if at himself.

"I didn't mean to tell you as much as I have, but you must understand the relationship to comprehend what has been happening. When my father killed himself some of his associates stepped in and saved the company. They were led by one of the finest people I've ever known. Boris Trueblood. He raised me. He sent me through school and then gave me a place with the company. He also took care of Austin and his mother and arranged for her to have an income until her death."

"Then I think Austin would be grateful."

"Grateful!" The word burst out of Gordon Merrill. "Grateful . . . you don't know my brother. He has twisted facts in his mind until he has convinced himself that Trueblood's group actually stole the company from us. He accepted every aid they gave him, and in each job the company assigned him to he managed to get himself into serious trouble."

"And you pulled him out?"

Merrill's shrug was expressive. "What else was I supposed to do? But he never tried anything like this before. I warned Trueblood not to put him in charge up here, but as soon as I was out of the country Austin persuaded him. Austin can be very persuasive when he chooses."

"I can see that, but I still do not see how he could steal the company."

Merrill sat tensely on the table's edge. "There was nothing difficult about stealing the gold itself. After all, the men who handle the bullion are all Austin's men. As for buying control of the company, the stock has been depressed in price during the past six months. We had difficulties in South America and Australia, and because the production here was cut to one third of last year's output the company has not paid a dividend. Austin's clique also started rumors that our Virginia City mines are played out."

"But why haven't Mr. Trueblood and his associates taken some action?"

"They did. They sent for me. But I was in the mountains in Colombia, trying to straighten out a silver property we'd bought down there. It took me five months to get home after the letter reached me."

"Well, and what do they hope to gain by holding you a prisoner?"

"Time. If they can hold me until after the stockholders' meeting they can vote Trueblood and his board of directors out of office and themselves in. Once they are in office, they figure, their troubles are over. The more immediate question is, what are they intending to do about you. They can't risk the chance that you might send a warning to San Francisco."

# CHAPTER NINE

Clarence Donovan followed Mary Campbell from the hotel. He stayed some distance behind the hurrying girl, fearful for her and fearful that if she realized he was there she would send him back.

When she hastened over the lip of the pit and headed for the office he stopped, then drifted along the main street to where a clump of trees grew along the depression's edge. From this vantage point some three hundred feet behind the mine building he watched the girl approach the group of men, saw it separate, saw Austin Cleaver come forward to her.

He had no idea of what was happening in the pit below him and watched Jean Armand move off without guessing that the head of the mine police was starting in search of him. Had he known he might have fled the camp, for his fear of Armand was even greater than his fear of Harmony Jones.

But he did not know, and he watched with surprise as the girl moved forward into the office. He waited for her to reappear, his nervousness growing, and when she did not come out by the end of an hour his panic was nearly uncontrollable.

But yet he waited, for he had not the slightest idea of what else to do. In the whole camp there was hardly anyone whom he knew or trusted. He even thought of Harmony, since the fat cook was a friend of Merrill's, but even in this extremity he could not bring himself to return to the bunkhouse. Instead, he started doubtfully back for the hotel.

He chose to take the littered alley which ran behind the stores fronting on Dayton's main street, and it was fortunate that he did so. Armand's police were already conducting a systematic search of the town for him.

He passed up the alley without being observed and came in through the kitchen door of the hotel. Hop Lee was at the iron sink and Jason Comstock stacking wood in the big box beside the range.

They both stopped to look up, and the old swamper said, "Armand didn't find you?"

"Find me?" The boy backed a step at the words. "Why should he want to find me?"

Jason Comstock wiped his mouth with the back of his hand. "I don't know. He was here a while ago looking for you. Then two of his men came, not ten minutes ago."

"But why . . . ?"

"Where's Miss Mary?"

The boy caught his breath, his mind centering on the girl, and he forgot some of his immediate fear in thinking about her.

"She went into the mine office. She didn't come out."

Jason Comstock blinked at him, trying to clear his drug-ridden senses. "Went in? Didn't come out? How long she been in there?"

"Over an hour."

"She might be just talking to Merrill. . . ."

"If he's a prisoner like you think would they let her stay there? Maybe they're holding her too."

The swamper swore. "I gotta get me a gun. No one's going to hurt that girl, no one while I'm around."

Clarence Donovan said cruelly, "Look at your hands. You couldn't hold a gun steady enough to fire one shot. Jean Armand would kill you before you got it out of the holster."

Park Campbell had come in from the dining room and stood listening to this last speech. He said now, "What's this talk about killing?"

Clarence Donovan swung around, excitement and worry making his high-pitched voice crack.

"They've got Mary."

"Who has Mary? Where?" The hotel man's usually unruffled calm was stirred a little by the boy's intensity.

"Austin Cleaver and Jean Armand."

"What do you mean, they've got her?"

The words spilled from Clarence then, and the hotel man's face turned grave as he listened. Finally he said weakly, "A bunch of nonsense. Cleaver wouldn't do anything like that."

"He's holding Merrill a prisoner. . . ."

"How do you know?"

Jason Comstock spoke. "Because I saw them take him from the hotel with a gun in his back last night." He told what he knew, and it began to make a pattern.

Park Campbell began cursing softly before the story was finished. He was not as a rule a profane man, but he was assailed now by a full sense of his own inadequacy, and his sudden anger was directed at himself.

"I'll see about this."

He swung and hurried through the door, but by the time he reached the lobby he paused, debating. To whom could he appeal? He ran over the list of merchants in his mind, discarding one after another. None of them would oppose Austin Cleaver and his mine police.

He thought of riding to the county seat but knew that he could never make the trip over the hazardous trail. In the end he did the one thing he should not have done. He went to the pit.

Austin Cleaver and Jean Armand saw him coming and walked slowly to meet him. They had been discussing Clarence Donovan, for Armand's men had reported that the boy could not be located within the town.

Park Campbell had fortified his courage with three quick drinks and his step was not quite steady, yet he came forward, unhesitating.

Cleaver watched him sardonically, saying to Armand, "Looks like we have another guest."

The Frenchman grunted. "If this keeps up we'll have to take over the hotel."

Cleaver looked at him. "You know, at times, Jean, you have an actually workable idea."

He stood waiting as Park Campbell approached.

"What do you want?"

There was a dignity in Park Campbell that all of the years of excesses had not erased. He was forced to raise his voice to compete with the monitor's roar, but his tone showed no feeling as he said, "My niece. She is not well. She should be at home, resting."

Cleaver bowed. "I am afraid that is impossible at this time. She will stay where she is until I decide what to do with her. Unfortunately she has mischievously concerned herself in my affairs."

Campbell told him tightly, "Then I will appeal for outside help."

Cleaver laughed. "Old man," he said, "you will do nothing. No one leaves town. Armand has men at the livery stable. Others are guarding the roads. Don't forget, this is a valley and there are only two roads out of it."

Campbell stood his ground. "I must at least make sure she is all right. I must see her."

"Why not?" Cleaver smiled thinly and stood aside.

After a moment's hesitation the hotel man moved forward into the office.

Merrill and the girl turned as he came in, and Mary said in quick surprise, "Uncle Park. What are you doing here?"

He closed the door carefully before he said

ruefully, "I came to get you. It seems it was a mistake."

"You mean you're a prisoner too?"

"It seems that the whole town is a prison. Cleaver has the roads and the livery stable guarded. I don't know how long he hopes to continue or what he's trying to do."

Gordon Merrill told him rapidly, "If he can keep me from getting word to San Francisco for the next thirty days he'll have accomplished what he wants."

Park Campbell raised his eyebrows. "Thirty days? Can he do it?"

Merrill shrugged. "No through road touches Dayton. No one comes here except the teamsters who bring in supplies. Who can stop him?"

They looked at each other through a long silence, then Merrill went on.

"How many people know why you came down here?"

Campbell's smile was twisted. "Jason Comstock and the Donovan kid."

Merrill shook his head. "No help there."

"But they simply can't keep us here for thirty days. Mary ought to be in bed right now."

"There's a bunk in the back room." Merrill turned to the girl. "I should have thought of it before."

"I'm all right." Mary rose from the desk chair. "This is ridiculous, that Austin Cleaver can rule this camp as if he were a Napoleon. He must know that sooner or later it will catch up with him."

Merrill grunted. "How? They'll be in control of the company. Certainly they won't prosecute themselves."

She shook her head slowly. "If I know anything at all about you, you'll not rest until you've settled accounts with him."

"If I'm alive."

She started to say, "You're joking," then checked herself. "You actually believe he would kill you? Your own brother would murder you?"

Merrill's lips warped down. "Austin won't do it himself, but either George Spain or Jean Armand will welcome the chance. They certainly won't let me walk out of here."

"But they would know that we would talk."

His look was more expressive than words, and she caught her breath.

"You mean that they might kill us too?"

He said quietly, "They are playing for very high stakes. The price of Magnus Mining Company stock is terribly depressed at the moment, but its resources are tremendous, and once the gold from this pit flows back

117

into company channels the stock will bound up on the exchange. It will double at least, perhaps triple. They stand to make millions of dollars, and they have never been men who let sentiment stand in the way of profit."

"So. But what are you going to do?"

He said, "Nothing, at the moment. If we only had someone outside, someone we could depend upon. . . ."

"There's Clarence."

His laugh was an unpleasant sound. "That kid is probably hiding under his bed. You'll get no help from him."

Clarence Donovan was hiding, but not under the bed. He was crouched in the clump of trees behind the mine office, having reached them by a circuitous route which avoided detection from the town. And he had a gun. He had taken Park Campbell's revolver from its place behind the hotel desk.

He could feel its weight in his pocket, and he was almost as afraid of it as he was of the guard who lounged in the shade of the distant building.

He did not know how to proceed from here. He waited, hoping each minute that the door would open and Mary Campbell would step out, free to return to the hotel.

But nothing like that happened. At noon one of Armand's men entered the office with a basket containing sandwiches. The afternoon dragged on. The stunning roar of the monitor mantling the pit seemed to shut the whole area off completely from the rest of the world.

Evening came and with it two new guards, one carrying blankets, the other a package of food.

The sun went down, the sky darkened, and the torches in the pit were lighted so that the work could go on.

Hunger made Clarence Donovan's stomach growl, but he did not shift his place. He lay there watching as lamplight rose to outline the rectangle of the office window.

He watched the two guards and presently saw them talking earnestly, then saw one move away toward the town.

The torches, flaming ten feet high, were arranged to illuminate the working face of the pit rather than the office, and while they cast their glow far enough to touch the front of the office clearly, the rear wall was in contrasting darkness.

Clarence Donovan drew a long, compulsive breath. He felt like a man about to leap into a pool of icy water. He pulled the gun from his pocket and, gripping it tensely in his thin hand, edged out from the shelter of the trees.

A match flared as the guard lit his pipe, then the man lounged out of view, around the side of the building nearest the pit. The boy stopped for a moment, then, gritting his teeth so hard that his jaws ached, he began to run forward.

One thing Clarence had always been able to do better than others was to run. His legs were long, and the persecution of his early youth had made him expert at escape.

He covered the hundred yards which separated the trees from the building in less than a minute and came against the dark wall panting. He stood, almost able to hear the quickened beat of his heart above the roar. Then he moved cautiously to the corner and, holding the gun ready, peered around it. The guard was not in sight.

He turned the corner and followed the side wall as far as the window and looked through. Merrill was sitting on the desk facing Park Campbell. Mary was not visible, since she was lying down on the bunk in the rear room.

The boy used the barrel of the gun to tap lightly on the glass. Merrill's head came about in a quick jerk. He stared for an instant at the long white face blurred by the dirty pane, then he glanced toward the door.

Then he was on his feet, crossing to the window in two leaps.

The sash stuck. It had not been opened for a long time, and he almost despaired of raising it before it moved upward in a sluggish, binding motion. As soon as the opening was wide enough Clarence thrust the gun into Merrill's waiting hand.

To Merrill nothing had ever felt quite so comforting as the smooth face plates of the old weapon. He turned it, spun the cylinder, balanced it in his palm, then swung around, thrusting it under his coat with his right hand, using his left to yank open the door.

The guard sat, his chair tilted back against the office wall, his pipe clenched between his thin lips. As the door opened he jumped from the chair, his hand snaking toward his own gun.

Merrill said quickly, "Will you send for Cleaver? Miss Campbell is sick."

The man came forward, his suspicion fading until too late. As he reached the door Merrill sneaked the gun from beneath his coat and rammed it against the man's stomach with a force that drove the wind out of him. He grunted and tried to back away, but Merrill's words were like a cutting whip.

"Get in here."

There was fear in the man's face as he obeyed, for he knew Merrill by reputation. Inside Merrill made him face the wall and swiftly lifted the holstered gun.

"Now get the belt off."

The guard unbuckled the cartridge belt sullenly.

"It won't do you no good." He was thinking of Jean Armand's anger and trying to save the situation. "They're waiting at the roads and livery. A grasshopper couldn't get out of Dayton."

Mary Campbell had appeared in the doorway of the back room and stood watching silently. Merrill was between the guard and the outside door and swung sharply as he heard it open.

Clarence Donovan burst in, his face flushed with the excitement of his temerity.

"You gotta hurry," he said hoarsely. "There was another guard. He went somewhere, but I'll bet he'll be back."

Merrill's eyes pierced into the boy. "Do you know, are the roads and the livery stable really guarded?"

"I . . . I guess so."

Merrill glanced at the two guns still in his hands. Mary saw the look.

"You're not going to try to shoot your way

out? You'll only be killed."

"Sure . . . that's right." The guard was still eager to regain his prisoner. "You haven't got a chance, Ghost. Armand has twenty men. Even you can't lick odds like that."

Park Campbell spoke. "Why don't you duck for those trees at the north end of the pit? Once you're in the hills they'd never catch you. Better take the boy with you. Armand will skin him if he gets his hands on him."

Clarence Donovan flinched at the words.

Merrill looked bleakly at the hotel man. Not only was Clarence Donovan in danger. Park Campbell and his niece were equally so. He had no illusions that her womanhood would save her life. To Austin Cleaver no person, male or female, was important if he constituted a threat to him.

And the girl and her uncle were a real threat. Of all the people in Dayton these would be the ones who could not be intimidated or coerced. They would talk. If he was murdered they would do their utmost to bring the killers to justice, and Cleaver well knew this.

He could not escape and leave them behind at the mercy of his half brother. Physically he could get away, yes. Morally he had no choice. He nodded.

"We'll all go."

Everyone in the room gaped at him, then the guard laughed.

"You'd never get away alone. How you going to take three cripples with you?"

Park Campbell's voice showed his anguish. "You're out of your mind. My niece isn't strong enough. She's ill and you know it."

Gordon Merrill had been making snap decisions all of his life, and he had made this one now. He looked toward the girl.

"What about it?"

Her face was very white save for the two patches of color on her smooth cheeks. He realized that they were put there by fever.

She lifted her head. "Whatever you say."

Merrill swung his eyes to Park Campbell and the boy. "Cleaver can't turn back now, he's committed too deeply. If any of us escape him he faces twenty to thirty years in prison. So do the men with him. Do you think you will be safe here?"

The girl spoke abruptly. "We will go. But how?"

"Through the drainage tunnel. It will take us out into the Canyon of the Bear."

He had turned to face her directly, and in that instant the guard made a dive for the door. Merrill caught the movement from the corner of his eye. He swung with the quickness of a panther, the gun in his hand coming up and down in a sharp chopping motion, clipping the side of the man's skull. He dropped as if he had been struck by a bolt of lightning.

In spite of herself Mary Campbell gasped. "You've killed him."

Merrill never even looked at the fallen man. He caught up the cartridge belt which the guard had let drop to the floor, strapped it about his flat hips, dropped one gun into the holster, and thrust the other under his belt buckle.

"Let's go."

Mary Campbell did not move. Her mind was racing. She thought, "He's like a well-trained animal, a mountain lion. He has no feeling. He doesn't care whether that man is alive or dead." A sense of revulsion rode up in her, and she almost cringed as Merrill caught her arm.

"Come."

She forced herself to move forward. He used his free hand to open the door. He glanced quickly around the pit. There was no one in sight except three workmen who with the help of the stone sled were dragging boulders away from the north end of the face and the two monitor men crouched beside the big nozzle where it sat like a cannon on its squat mounting. They were working at the south end of the face, two hundred feet from the entrance to the shaft.

"Run."

Merrill locked his hand under the girl's arm and half carried her across the broken ground, Campbell and Clarence at his heels.

# CHAPTER TEN

Harmony Jones came up Main Street looking for all the world like one of the Civil War balloons on legs. He turned in at the Pit saloon and went directly toward the bar.

From habit the bartender slid the proper bottle before him, and he filled the small glass, carrying it to his lips and drinking with his accustomed relish.

"You haven't seen that Donovan kid around, have you?"

The bartender shook his head.

"The damn brat."

"Jean Armand's been looking for him all afternoon. I guess maybe he left town."

Harmony showed his surprise. "And what would Jean be wanting with the likes of him?"

The bartender shrugged. He had served drinks through most of his adult life and had long since learned that the easiest way to stay alive was not to be curious about anything.

"I didn't ask him."

Jason Comstock was cleaning one of the cuspidors. It was the slow hour. Only three salesmen were clustered at the bar's far end, and but one poker table was running. The swamper replaced the cuspidor, waiting until the bartender moved away, then sidled up to Harmony.

Harmony shook his head. "Nothing doing."

"I wasn't cadging a drink." The old man sounded offended. "You're a friend of Gordon Merrill's, aren't you? A good friend?"

The fat rolls of Harmony's face made his eyes seem smaller than they really were, and they almost disappeared as he squinted down.

"So I'm a good friend of the Ghost. What do you want from him?"

"I don't want nothing." Jason Comstock was getting mad. It was a luxury he had nearly forgotten. "You big tub of lard, I'm just trying to help him. And he needs help bad."

Harmony threw his head back and laughed. "That's a hot one. Ghost Merrill needing help from you. Wait until he hears that."

"If somebody don't do something quick

he ain't going to hear nothing much again."

The fat man set the glass on the bar, the laughter suddenly gone from his eyes as he realized that this was not a joke.

"Well, out with it."

Jason Comstock told him hurriedly. "If you don't believe me go over to the hotel and see if Park Campbell or his niece are there."

Harmony Jones blinked at the bottle on the bar. He reached out, filled the glass, started to pick it up, then shoved it toward Comstock.

"Here."

The swamper lifted the glass. Harmony drank from the neck of the bottle. He wiped his thick lips on the back of his hand.

"Who else knows about this?"

"The China cook at the hotel and young Donovan."

Harmony stiffened. "Where is he? The kid?"

"I don't know. He ducked out right after Campbell took off for the pit."

Harmony grunted and turned out of the saloon. There were few people on the street, and he plowed ahead, hesitating for a moment before the hotel, then deciding that he would only be wasting time by stopping. He moved on toward the pit.

He reached its edge in time to see Merrill and his companions emerge from the office and run toward the shaft house. He shouted to them, but the monitor drowned out even his bull-like voice.

He started after them, then stopped, realizing what they were about. He swore softly, hesitated a moment longer, then turned and hurried back to the bunkhouse.

In its kitchen he hastily caught up a burlap sack and began shoving food into it. Of one thing he was certain, the fugitives were heading into the hills and they had no food, for there could not have been any in the office.

Gordon Merrill was also considering food at the moment, along with other problems. Climbing down the hundred-foot ladder to the level of the drainage tunnel, he wondered how long it would be before Cleaver discovered their escape, how soon Jean Armand's men would be on their trail. Not long enough, he felt sure.

Below him, in the uncertain light of the miner's lamp which he had picked up in the shaft house and fastened about her head, the girl's face showed the strain as she lowered herself step by painful step.

Her uncle was below her, Clarence Donovan next. The descent took a good five minutes, for the girl moved with agonizing slowness.

At times it seemed to her that she would never reach the bottom. Her arms ached, and she was attacked by recurring spells of dizziness. But the rope fastened under her arms and about Merrill's middle was a source of comfort, and despite the aversion she had experienced when he struck down the guard she knew a warm glow at his thoughtfulness.

Finally her feet touched the catwalk edging the ditch at the bottom of the shaft. She grasped the ragged rock of the wall, overcome by the certainty that she would faint.

Her uncle moved quickly forward, but Merrill dropped to her side and his arm was strong about her shoulders, steadying her.

"Fine," he said. "Can you keep going?" His voice was far away under the drowning sound that engulfed them.

She tried to speak and could not for a long minute. Then she nodded.

"Just let me catch my breath. This is silly. . . . If I'd been climbing . . ."

He loosened the rope from beneath her arms, and she looked about her.

Water and gravel poured out of the shaft's pentstock in a breath-taking rush. The noise in the narrow confines of the tunnel was a curious thing, not as loud as she would have expected but a continuing roar that washed over them and deadened every other sound.

Merrill said, "All right." He spoke easily, with no show of tension, still in the faraway tone. He turned to Clarence Donovan. "Help her. I'm going ahead. There are guards."

He moved off, sure-footed though he carried no light, one hand on the wall at his side to steer his course, the other on the grip of his holstered gun.

She watched him fade into the shadows of the tunnel ahead, beyond the radius of her tiny lamp, watched him go with an increasing dread which she could not crowd down.

Clarence Donovan came forward hesitantly to put a hand under her arm, to steer her along the catwalk slowly. The boy, she realized, was very conscious of her physically, very embarrassed at touching her. It gave her a warm feeling for him. He was so terribly shy, so utterly inexperienced.

The boards beneath their feet were damp with spray from the roiling waters in the ditch, rough and uneven and slippery. She did not know how far they went. She did not know that the tunnel was a mile and a half long. She lost track of time. Her legs turned rubbery, and at length she was forced to call a halt.

She sank down on the wet walk and rested her head against the rock wall, closing her eyes, nauseated. The man and the boy looked at her, then at each other, helplessly.

Park Campbell longed for a drink. It had been many years since he had gone for more than four waking hours without the help of alcohol. His hand shook as he reached down and touched her shoulder.

"It's only a little farther."

She turned her face up to him with the expression of a sick child reaching for the security of her family protection.

"I can't."

He said to the boy, "Give me a hand," and together they lifted her to her feet.

Supporting her on either side, they made their unsteady progress. They had edged on perhaps a quarter of a mile when the shot rang out above the water's growl. It was followed by a second, a third.

The girl froze, then with a surge of renewed energy she shook loose and was running forward, calling, "Gordon. Gordon," hysterically.

Gordon Merrill could not hear her. He was crouched down behind the corner of the so-called gold room.

This was a square room cut from the rock

at the side of the tunnel. It had been fitted with a thick plank door secured by a heavy lock passed through hasps set in the door and in the stone. In this room during the cleanup periods were stored the buckets of gold amalgam as they were gathered from the riffles of the sluice.

After the cleanup was completed they were carted above ground to be retorted and run into bars.

At present, since it was not cleanup time, the door was not fastened, and the guards, on duty at all times in the tunnel, used it as a place to sit.

There were three of them. One was supposed to be at his post at the exit where the tunnel opened into the canyon. But the night was cold and he had retreated to the gold room. He and his fellows now played cards by the light of a smoke-streaked lantern.

Merrill had seen the glow as he advanced along the catwalk. He moved on to the half open door, his gun in his hand. He tried to ease the panel shut, meaning to slide the chain in place and thus imprison the guards. It would give him a few hours' start, for the shift would not change until morning.

But one of the men looked up at the wrong moment. His move was purely instinctive. He jumped to his feet, drawing as he rose, and sent a bullet crashing into the door, making Merrill leap back for shelter.

Both other guards were instantly on their feet, and both fired, the slugs drawing long grooves in the heavy planks.

Then there was silence in the tunnel save for the roar of the rushing water.

Merrill called above the roar, "Throw your guns out. You haven't any choice."

There was silence within, then a voice called back. "Who is it?"

"Gordon Merrill."

"I don't believe it."

"Stick your head out and you'll get a bullet through it."

There was a conference within. Merrill could not hear what was said, but he heard their voices raised in argument, and he smiled grimly to himself. He could picture what was in their minds. They were trying to decide whether to rush him, for their fear of his reputation was not greater than their fear of what Jean Armand would do when their chief learned that they had let someone slip unobserved into the tunnel.

"Throw them out. You've got one minute before I start shooting."

One gun thudded onto the catwalk, slid across it and dropped into the ditch with a small splash. Then a second came and finally a third, the last two staying on the rough boards.

"Now your belts."

The belts writhed through the air and landed solidly.

"Now hand me out the lantern."

One man appeared in the doorway and set the lantern gingerly outside. He straightened, staring out at the white-haired engineer.

"Close the door."

Fear leaped into the man's dark eyes, and panic touched his voice.

"You ain't going to lock us in here to starve?"

"Stop whining. You won't starve." Contempt was heavy in Merrill's tone. "The morning shift will turn you loose."

"And Armand will skin us alive. You got our guns, let us cut out."

"Back up."

The man hesitated, then he risked a step forward. Merrill's shot whipped between his legs and chipped stone from the floor behind him. He jumped back quickly. Merrill pushed the thick door shut, snapped the chain through the hasps, and closed the lock.

He was turning to pick up the guns and

belts when Mary Campbell stumbled forward.

"Gordon. Gordon. Are you safe?"

She saw that he was. She collapsed against him, her hands biting into his shoulders, the miner's lamp slipping from her head to fall to the floor, extinguishing itself.

He held her, looking down at her upturned face. Her breathing was very rapid, very shallow. Her eyes were closed, and he thought for an instant that she was dying, and remembered another girl whom he had held in his arms in another tunnel a long time ago.

"Mary . . ." His voice was not steady. "Mary . . ."

Her eyes opened, and a tiny embarrassed smile tugged at her lips. "I . . . I just ran too fast. I thought maybe . . ." The words trailed off.

"That I was dead?"

She shivered. It was a word she did not like. She had come far too close to death herself for it to be a pleasant thought.

"I didn't know. I heard the guns . . ."

She broke off as her uncle and Clarence Donovan ran up, and said before they could speak, "I'm all right."

She was not all right. She found when they started forward that she was too weak with exhaustion to walk.

Merrill handed a gun and a belt each to the boy and the hotel man. He motioned Clarence to take the lantern and stooping, caught the girl up in his arms, cradling her as if she were but a baby.

She was too weary to protest, to even care. So, with the boy in the lead lighting the way and Park Campbell bringing up the rear, they reached the mouth of the tunnel and looked out southward, across the deep canyon of the Yuba River, across the distant, tree-covered ridges that rode away from them in mile upon mile of empty land.

Far below them the river was a twisting snake of moving water glinting in the moonlight. On their immediate left the sluice spewed out its load of sand and gravel to drop away in a man-made waterfall down the sheer canyon side.

To their right a wide road had been cut along the canyon's face. It had been built at the time the tunnel was driven, for the use of the workmen and their supplies. It rose from the tunnel's yawning entrance to the rim of the canyon high above them, half a mile in a steep grade. Thence it ran westward along the rim four miles and there joined with the bisecting road which connected Dayton and Grass Valley.

The Dayton–Grass Valley road was the only possible crossing of the Yuba within thirty miles. Winding north from Grass Valley it descended into the mile-deep canyon in a series of switchbacks, crossed the swirling river on a wooden bridge, climbed the north slope, and twisted on to Dayton, five miles beyond its juncture with the mine's haulage road.

Merrill knew every foot of the terrain through which they would need to travel. He had conducted all the preliminary surveys himself. In this knowledge was embodied the awareness that they were in a natural trap.

Cleaver's men had only to ride out the Grass Valley road to the canyon and turn eastward along the haulage road to meet them. The horses could cover the distance in a little over an hour.

Even if they reached the rim safely they had few choices of direction. If they continued west along the road Cleaver would surely come upon them. If they turned back east they headed into rough, unsettled country, no towns, no telegraph lines. South their path was blocked by the gash of the canyon. North would lead them up Dohne Mountain and eventually back into Dayton.

And Austin Cleaver had to see that they did not break through this trap.

# CHAPTER ELEVEN

Carrying his well-filled sack in one big hand, a rifle in the other, Harmony Jones hurried back to the pit. There was no sign of the fugitives, no unusual activity, and no one noticed him as he hastened across to the shaft house.

Inside he paused, panting. Harmony had not hurried so in twenty years. He looked with disfavor at the deep, dark hole, gathering himself.

Harmony had lived around mining operations for many years, but he had never liked it underground. He had a fear of dark, closed places, and it was all he could do to force himself to pick up one of the miner's lamps from the high shelf, fill it, and fasten it to the front of his hat.

Then, slinging his rifle over his shoulder by a bit of cord tied to its stock and barrel, he carried the heavy sack to the mouth of the shaft and pitched it into the blackness.

He could not hear it land. The falling water in the second compartment blotted out all other sound.

He climbed down. To him the climb felt hours long, but he made better time than Merrill and his companions had.

At the bottom he found the sack. It had burst open, spilling flour and beans. He gathered up what he could, tied the sack together with the cord that had held his rifle, and started along the tunnel. He was not too careful. He figured that Merrill had already disposed of the guards and was not surprised when he met no one.

He reached the far opening and turned unhesitating into the haulage road. There was no other way to go, for the canyon dropped abruptly from the tunnel mouth in an incline that no human could hope to negotiate.

The track was rutted deep into the stone by the many iron tires of the supply wagons. Harmony had worked on the tunnel job, running the bunkhouse built in a side canyon about a mile west of the work area, and he knew the territory over which he traveled almost as well as did Gordon Merrill.

From the old bunkhouse several paths led out. A man could climb any one of them and lose himself in the virgin timber of the higher slopes. It was Harmony's fear that Merrill would reach the old building and be gone before he caught them.

He broke into a lumbering run. The thin mountain air was oxygen light and his lungs began to labor. His huge paunch jarred up and down with his effort.

He had to stop. His heart was hammering so loudly that he feared it would pound a hole in his rib cage. He laid the bag of food on the ground, stood the rifle against the bank, and sat down on a rock that had rolled from the mountainside above.

The moon was a disk halfway up the distant sky, outlining the serried rows of peaks above him. Harmony could not understand what was troubling him. And then he knew. For months he had lived with the roar of the monitors. Day and night the surging stream of water had sent out its blasting fog of sound to submerge everything about the pit. But here the intervening mountain chain cut out the man-made din. The only sound that reached his ears was that of the water pouring from the tunnel. And even this was muted by distance and trees. Then he began hearing the ordinary night sounds of the hills for the first time in many a day.

Suddenly he laughed. He was feeling freer than he had for years. He wondered what would happen in the Dayton bunkhouse in the morning. He grinned. The day shift would crawl from their blankets and head shivering toward the dining room for breakfast. Failing to find it on the table, they would invade the kitchen.

The stove would be cold. No hot water. No food. He could hear their curses vividly, for it was common practice in any mining camp to blame the cook for everything including bad weather.

Without realizing what he was doing he began to sing. He rose from his seat on the rock, gathered up the bag and rifle, and plodded on up the steep slant of the rising road.

His voice made up in volume what it lacked in music, and it filled the night, echoing back from the blank faces of the canyon as if all the weird spirits of the mountains hastened to join his chorus.

Gordon Merrill heard it.

They had paused at the old bunkhouse to rest. The place was no longer used and was already falling into ruin. The thick log walls stood, but the window lights were broken and heavy snow packs had caved the shake roof.

144

He had built a fire in the rusting stove, and they huddled around it, the girl too exhausted to speak. Park Campbell sullenly nursed the clamor his nerves made for alcohol. The boy was restless.

Merrill was disappointed. He had hoped that the place was still visited at least by the tunnel guards, that there would be food staples there, coffee, flour, perhaps beans.

There was nothing. Industriously the pack rats had carted away everything portable, exchanging it for whatever they had carried in, perhaps precious to them but to man useless bits of sticks and stone.

The fire felt warm against the mountain chill, but Merrill stood in the doorway studying the ridges above him, trying to decide on the best path for his purpose.

Behind him dipped the deep canyon, nearly impossible to cross. He would have chosen to head south, across the Yuba, since there were a dozen settlements within a fifty-mile radius. From any of these he could have secured horses and a certain amount of protection. But the canyon barred that route. Alone, he might have attempted the descent, but he knew that the others could never make it, and he could not bring himself to leave them.

To the north across the mountains lay

Dayton. To the west was the winding trail to Grass Valley and Nevada City. This was the first area Cleaver and Jean Armand would cover. The natural assumption would be that anyone trying to escape would head west to cut this trail and cross the canyon on it.

That left the east to climb, climb toward the towering peaks, climb until the canyon narrowed enough to be crossed. He had surveyed for some thirty miles above the tunnel and had found no such crossing. But he had little choice.

Food concerned him, but not too greatly. At this time of year the deer were still not too high in the hills, and a man who knew what he was doing should be able to find meat enough. He would have been more confident had he had a rifle, but with luck he should be able to catch them at a watering place and knock one down with a revolver.

And then he heard the burst of Harmony's singing. For an instant he tensed, not recognizing the discord. Then he relaxed. There could not possibly be two such unlyrical voices in the whole country.

"Harmony. . . ."

He shouted it aloud, and the sudden shout shocked the group around the stove. Ignoring them, he dashed from the doorway and ran along the grass-grown path from the bunkhouse to the trail.

He saw the cook's enormous figure, grotesque in the moonlight. For a moment he thought that Harmony was injured, bent almost double, then he made out the bulging sack on the thick shoulders.

"Harmony. Where in hell did you come from?"

The singing died, and there was relief in the bull-toned bellow.

"Ghost. Where are you?"

"Up here. Toward the bunkhouse."

Harmony turned, peering upward. He swore noisily, then lumbered up the steep path.

"Darned if I didn't nearly miss it." He panted to a stop at Merrill's side, swinging the loaded sack down thankfully.

"What have you got there?"

"Grub."

"How did you know where we were?"

Harmony grunted, breathed himself like a spent horse, then in short, spaced sentences told of the conversation in the saloon.

Merrill began to chuckle. "It beats all. If Austin had ever treated Comstock as though he were half human none of us would be here. He'd still have me. It was Comstock who told them at the hotel where I was, and if Cleaver loses the mine it will be thanks to Comstock."

The cook mopped his forehead with a tree trunk forearm. "What you talking? What's he want you for? What's he up to?"

The quick explanation made Harmony whistle. Merrill finished, saying, "If I can get word to Trueblood before that stockholders' meeting, Cleaver's stopped."

"Think you can?"

Merrill looked at him speculatively. "You could. You can get through, they wouldn't stop you. Climb the mountain behind this camp and follow the crest down to the Grass Valley road. At Grass Valley telegraph Trueblood in my name."

The cook backed off, groaning. "I ain't much for climbing mountains, Gordon, and you know it. But that ain't it. They'd hang me. When they find I ain't at the bunkhouse they'll be suspicious. When they find I walked out with all the grub I could lay my hands on, and stole one of Jean Armand's rifles at that . . ." He let the words trail off unhappily. Plainly the mine police would not let him pass.

Gordon Merrill nodded acceptance. Harmony Jones was right in that he would be suspect, and the cook was not noted for physical bravery.

"All right. We'll all head east. It's about all we can do, and we have to get out of here."

He turned toward the bunkhouse, carrying the sack while Harmony trailed him with the rifle. As they came through the door the three inside watched then: nervously. At sight of the cook Clarence Donovan let out a gasp like the squeak of a frightened mouse. Harmony spotted him at the same moment, and his roar of anger shook the room.

"So there you are. . . ." He took one convulsive step forward, unconsciously bringing the rifle to his shoulder.

Gordon Merrill knocked it aside. "You lost your mind?"

Harmony's growl was aggrieved. "That little stinker ran out on me, after I fed him, after I bought him clothes."

"Lucky for us he did. He got us out of the pit office."

Harmony looked unbelieving. "How was that?"

Merrill told him. Harmony stared, dumfounded. "The kid did that? Honest? I didn't think he had the nerve to stand up to his own shadow."

Mary Campbell spoke positively. "You don't know him. Clarence is just as brave as

149

anyone else."

Harmony opened his mouth to protest, then closed it slowly. "If you say so, ma'am." He shrugged, looking to Merrill. "So, what's the orders?"

"We move," said Merrill. "I want to be five miles up canyon by daylight."

He went to the stove, putting out the fire. Behind him the girl caught her lower lip between her teeth. She was more tired than she had been since her trip west, and the thin air of the high altitude was forcing her lungs to excessive effort, but she said nothing. Park Campbell said softly to Harmony, "You wouldn't have a bit of whiskey in that tote sack?"

The big cook started to say no, then he saw how Campbell's hands were shaking. He found the flat pint in his coat pocket, removed the cork, and extended it to the hotelkeeper.

"One swallow," he said. "You take more than that and I'll break your neck. It may have to last a long time."

Park Campbell took the bottle. He tilted it, aware that Harmony watched him with the attention of a hawk. He swallowed once and lowered the bottle regretfully.

The cook took it from his hand, hesitated, then recorked it without bringing it to his own lips.

Merrill had moved to the girl. "Ready?"

She nodded. "You aren't going to carry me again. You can't possibly carry me clear across the mountains."

A glint of grim humor touched his lips. "I'd better be able to."

He stooped. He caught her behind the knees so that she sat across his forearm, her body resting against his shoulder, her arm around his neck to steady herself.

She knew that her cheeks had flushed, and not from the fever. To be thus carried by a man, especially a man whom she barely knew, was an act she would never have dreamed of before she came west.

She was strongly aware of him, of his easy strength, of the sure way he moved on the rough ground. She could not see his face in the night. She lay back against his shoulder, trying to make it as easy for him as she could.

She wondered what his thoughts were. She knew that her breast was pressed against his cheek, and the thought increased her unease.

Merrill led out, moving up an overgrown path that seemingly had not been used by man for years. It rose sharply to top a small hogback that ran up out of the side canyon toward the rim above them.

Clarence Donovan came close behind. He had taken up the bag from the unprotesting cook and was bent beneath its weight, panting as he climbed, his narrow chest fighting for sufficient oxygen in the light air. Park Campbell followed him, and Harmony with his rifle kept the rear.

The sky ahead was beginning to lighten, and the change which is the difference between night and day touched the woods around them.

Gordon Merrill stopped at the hogback and set the girl gently to the ground. She had a look at his face in the growing light and saw the dullness of fatigue in his eyes.

"If only I hadn't come back to the pit . . ."

He said, "You did." He said it flatly. "Never look back, Mary. What has happened has happened. Nothing changes it." He turned away then, and she realized that he was referring to his wife.

Suddenly she was angry. She respected grief as she respected any emotion, but to allow a ten-year-old tragedy to warp your whole existence was the thinking of a fool. Yet she knew that Gordon Merrill was not a fool. She faced him squarely.

"That isn't true, Gordon. I tried to help and only made things worse. If I weren't

152

here you'd be a lot farther away from Dayton than you are now. You might even have crossed the canyon. Isn't that right?"

Unwillingly he said, "It is."

"Then you must go. With the food Harmony brought we can hide in this timber for a few days while you get your word out to San Francisco and bring back help. You can't carry me clear across the mountains. No one could."

He debated.

Clarence Donovan said unexpectedly, "She's right, Mr. Merrill. You go on. I'll stay here and take care of her."

Merrill looked from one to the other. Of the group he had faith only in Harmony to succeed. The fat cook had been raised in a hard school, and he knew the rules of survival in this land.

"What about it?" He spoke to Harmony.

The cook pushed the broken hat far back on his big head and ran a thick hand through his uncut hair.

"Seems like they got a point. We ain't all going to get loose, tramping through these hills. You might as well travel with a herd of elephants."

Merrill looked about them. "I can't leave you here."

Harmony shook his head. "No, not here.

But remember, there's a box canyon with a spring over on Dohne's Peak. We'd have water and we'd have grub and we'd be kinda out of the way."

"That's off on the old trail, the one that leads north from the bunkhouse."

"And it's back toward Dayton. Cleaver won't figure we'd double back. He'll figure we'd head up canyon to the headwaters to try to cross it there."

Merrill looked at him silently. "All right. We'll have to cut back and pick up the other trail." He stooped to lift the girl.

"I can walk. You're nearly worn out now."

He ignored the protest. He swung her up and, turning, started back down the trail, feeling the warmth of her body against his own, feeling the soft mound of her breast against his cheek. He glanced back. The others were arguing as to who would carry the sack of food.

He turned his head, and suddenly the girl's face was close to his. Without thought he kissed her. He heard her tiny gasp of surprise and felt her stiffen for an instant as if she would force herself out of his arms.

Then his lips were warm on hers, and the struggle went out of her, but she was not limp. Her arm tightened about his neck, bringing his head lower against hers.

# CHAPTER TWELVE

Austin Cleaver was notified of the prisoners' escape at two-thirty in the morning, just as Harmony Jones was pushing along the trail in his effort to catch Merrill.

He had been playing poker in the back room of the Pit saloon. He had been losing and was already in a thoroughly ill humor.

Jean Armand hurried in and stopped between Cleaver and George Spain. Cleaver was aware of his arrival, but he did not speak until the hand was played out and he had again lost. Then he tossed the offending cards into the middle of the table and pushed back his chair, looking up at Armand.

"Want my place?"

The mine policeman was nervous. He leaned over Cleaver. "Merrill's gone." He said it in a low whisper that carried only to Cleaver and Spain.

"Gone?" Cleaver stared up at him, unable

to believe his ears. George Spain had picked up the discards and begun to shuffle the deck. He froze.

Armand said, "Let's get out of here."

Cleaver rose, not even bothering to cash in the chips still stacked before him. George Spain was more prudent. He waited until the houseman paid him before he trailed them into the street.

They stood under the wooden awning before the restaurant next door to the Pit. The restaurant was deserted and dark, and there was no one in sight on the street.

"How'd he get away?"

There was no trace of feeling in Cleaver's voice. At times he could be as childish as a baby with a tantrum, at others he could be coldly unemotional, and this he was now.

"We don't know exactly. I left Bill Phipps and Al McCord on guard. Al left. When he got back he found Bill unconscious on the office floor."

"Where'd McCord go?"

"Well, his girl was sick and . . ."

"Fire him." Cleaver turned and started to walk toward the mine.

"I already have." Jean Armand had to hurry to catch up. George Spain followed rapidly.

"Have you checked the guards?"

"Yeah. He didn't use the roads and he didn't get a horse from the livery."

"The girl and her father?"

"Gone too."

Cleaver stopped incredulously. "He took them with him?"

"Looks like it."

"The damn fool." A fleeting, vicious grin crossed Cleaver's thin mouth. "Alone he might have made it before we could head him off. With that drag he hasn't a chance. Get your men and get them riding."

"I've already sent to the bunkhouse. They're all to meet us at the office."

There were two men already there when Cleaver arrived: the guard whom Merrill had knocked out, seated in a chair, and Vic Parker, the company doctor, bandaging the bruised head. Cleaver did not so much as glance at the guard. He looked at the doctor.

"How bad is he?"

Parker shrugged. "He's got an inch gash in his scalp. He's lucky to be alive."

"Can he talk?"

"He can try. He's still woozy."

"Give him a slug of whiskey."

"That's the last thing he needs right now."

Austin Cleaver's control slipped. Millions of dollars were sliding through his fingers, and the chance of a long prison term loomed directly before him, and this fool prattled about not giving the idiot who had let Merrill escape a slug of whiskey.

"God damn it, do as I tell you." He half raised his hand as if to strike the doctor.

Parker glared back at him, but there was no nerve in the man. Whiskey and insecurity had made him a company doctor in the first place, and an illegal operation in the east had sent him fleeing into these barren hills.

He pulled his own bottle from his hip pocket and held it to the guard's dry lips. The man swallowed convulsively twice, then strangled. Whiskey and saliva leaked from the corner of his slack mouth. He rested his elbows on his knees. His head hung forward, and a dry retching shook his body. Cleaver pushed him erect.

"All right. What happened?"

The man's eyes rolled. "He . . . he had a gun."

"Who? Merrill? . . . Where'd he get it?"

"The boy brought it. He . . . sneaked up behind the shack and shoved it through the window."

Cleaver swore. "I told all of you to watch that window."

He slapped the man's cheek, and the head rolled sidewise. The doctor took half a step forward but stopped as Cleaver threw a baleful glance in his direction.

"Where'd they go?"

The guard's head had fallen on his chest again. Cleaver grabbed him by the hair and jerked his head up.

"Where'd they go?"

"The drainage tunnel."

Cleaver released the hair. The head dropped. Cleaver swung around, glaring at Armand.

"That's one you didn't think of."

Jean Armand was not cowed by Austin Cleaver as were the others. For all his faults Armand was seldom cowed by anyone. The lone exception had been Gordon Merrill, and the memory burned in his mind now.

"You didn't think of it either. We haven't time to start arguing. We've got to get after them."

Cleaver nodded sharply. They turned out of the office. Cleaver stood for a minute staring at the shaft house as if in some way it was fully responsible for Merrill's escape.

"George." He turned to Spain. "Take two men and go out through the tunnel. If he hasn't killed the guards, take them with you. They had to go up the haulage road outside. There's no other way."

Spain nodded.

"He can't be moving very fast, with that girl." Cleaver swung toward Armand and behind him saw the guards break from the bunkhouse and come running.

"Jean, take the rest of your crew and horses, extra horses. Have Harmony fix you all up with grub. Then cut down the Grass Valley road. Send two men on to guard the bridge. Merrill's bound to try to cross it. You go on and meet George, and whatever you do, don't let Merrill get to a telegraph line." He turned full circle. The guards were grouped about him now. "A thousand dollars gold to the man who finds Merrill and kills him."

They grinned back at him in silence. Jean Armand had recruited them from the scum of the mining camps, and there was not one among them who was not wanted for some crime in some distant town.

"All right. Get going. And Jean, remember, everything's riding on you now."

As they returned toward the bunkhouse Cleaver went back into the office. The injured guard still lolled in his chair. The doctor was in the act of draining his bottle. Cleaver looked him over sardonically.

"If I didn't need you, Doc, I'd toss you out on your behind. I hope I never get sick when you're the only doctor around."

Vic Parker tossed the empty bottle into the waste basket and turned his red-rimmed eyes on the mine boss.

"I hope so too. It would be more temptation than I could withstand, and I've never intentionally killed a man yet."

"There's always a first time." Cleaver jerked his head toward the injured guard. "Get him out of here."

The doctor looked startled. "Where do you want me to take him?"

"I don't care. Just get him out of my sight."

The seated man struggled to his feet and stood weaving. He said in an uncertain voice, "I've done your dirty work for years, Cleaver. Now I'm through."

"You're all through," said Cleaver, and made a mental note to tell Armand that this one had to be taken care of, he was the kind who would talk.

He watched the guard lurch out, followed by the doctor, then he sat down heavily at the desk. Suddenly he was very tired. Until Merrill had showed up at Dayton everything had been moving according to his plan, and since his brother's arrival nothing had worked.

He hated Gordon Merrill. He had always hated him, and through the years that hatred had grown into an obsession. He was one of those who seldom blamed failure on his own shortcomings, and he did not blame himself now. The failure was in the men who worked for him, not in himself.

The door behind him opened, and he started up to see Jean Armand step tensely into the opening, and the anger that rode him was brittle in his voice.

"I thought you'd ridden out."

Armand's own anger was controlled. "I thought you'd like to know that Harmony's gone."

Cleaver blinked at him almost stupidly.

"And one of my rifles is missing, plus a lot of grub."

Cleaver considered this, and his lips thinned back over his teeth.

"You think he went with Merrill?"

"He's a good friend of Gordon's, you know that. I warned you not to keep him on."

Cleaver's temper got completely away from him. "You warned me. You warned me. Everyone's always warning me. So the fat louse went with them. What difference does it make?"

"It means that they have food."

"I don't care what they've got. Just make certain that Merrill doesn't get south of the

162

canyon. Now move."

Armand had known Cleaver for ten years. He was used to the man's unpredictable moods and erratic tantrums, but he had never seen him so near the ragged edge as he appeared at this moment. He said coldly, "You'd better get a grip on yourself. One of these days you're going to talk like that to the wrong man."

He stepped out of the door then, closing it very softly behind him. Cleaver stared at the panel, the tide of anger gradually washing out of him, to be replaced by a sullen determination.

He rose. He lifted the gun from its holster and checked the cylinders, then he opened the door and crossed the pit to the shaft house.

Climbing down the ladder in the small patch of radiance which his lamp made, he wondered what he intended doing. He had not planned to join the manhunt personally, but he was too restless to sit and wait.

He did not hurry. He knew that he would reach the Yuba side long before Armand and his riders could make the circuitous trip by the wagon trail. He found the bottom and moved along the catwalk, listening to the rush of water below him, picturing in his mind's eye the gold constantly accumulating behind the riffles.

It was all his. His and George Spain's and his associates' in San Francisco.

He thought of his brokers there, the men who had used his stolen gold to secretly buy up the Magnus stock. He meant to use them as front men, not to appear in the company himself for at least two or three years. Instead he would stay on as manager of the Dayton pit.

He came to the tunnel's mouth having seen no one, and after pausing there a moment turned up the road toward the old bunkhouse. As soon as he stepped into the side canyon he was challenged, and one of the men who had gone with George Spain melted out of the shadows to stand exposed in the growing morning light.

"Oh. I didn't recognize you."

"Where's Spain?"

"Up at the old bunkhouse. We're waiting for the horses."

Cleaver nodded and passed the man, going on up to the log building. He had not stopped to bring a heavy coat, and he shivered in the early chill.

The bunkhouse door was ajar and the fallen roof section let in the cold, but the stove was a cherry red and sent welcome waves of heat over the wreckage of the place.

George Spain stood with his back to the stove, his blocky body looking thicker than usual in the sheepskin coat. He showed surprise when Cleaver came in, then as the mine boss came on to the stove he said, "Thought you were going to stay in town."

Cleaver grunted. "I got restless. Any sign of them?"

"We haven't seen them, but they've been here. The stove was still warm when we came in."

"Which way did they go?"

Spain's shrug was expressive. "We're waiting for daylight to find out. Anyhow, we can't move far until Jean gets here with the horses."

Cleaver's mouth drew down at the corners. Spain saw the look. He was a solid unimaginative man who seldom lost his temper or his sense of balance.

"Take it easy. Well get him. He can't get out. He's saddled with an old drunk, a dumb kid, and a sick girl. Where can he hope to go? I don't think he can cross the main canyon, but even if he managed it he couldn't take those people with him."

"And a fat cook," Cleaver added. "Don't ask me why or how, but Harmony Jones is with him, with food and a rifle."

George Spain rubbed his nose thoughtfully. "That changes things a little. We'd better round them up as soon as possible. I'd figured there was no real hurry, that hunger would drive them out of the bushes in twenty-four hours. As soon as Jean gets here with the horses and it's light enough to pick up the trail, we'll move. But we better grab a bite to eat first. It may take several hours to dig them out of the timber."

It was more than several hours. Armand arrived twenty minutes after Cleaver's appearance. He had sent two men across the bridge to the canyon's south rim, with orders to patrol it in case by some miracle Merrill managed to cross. Two more he left guarding the main road so that Merrill could not descend its twisting turns into the canyon.

He still had nine with him, and these, coupled with the released mine guards, with Spain and Cleaver and those who had come through the tunnel with Spain, gave them seventeen. Certainly that should be enough to comb the country thoroughly.

While the men fixed breakfast Armand took a long look outside.

The trails leading away from the bunkhouse were little better than deer tracks. They had been created by the tunnel workers during their occupation in the area, for they had had little recreation save hunting.

One track led eastward, paralleling the rim of the big canyon, and this bore marks of recent use. But after following the marks for nearly a mile Armand came to the point where Merrill had turned back.

He retraced his way to the log building where the bulk of the men were eating a hasty breakfast, and tried the track north. After a few hundred feet he was sure he was on the trail of the fugitives. The print of a woman's shoe, made where Merrill had set the girl down for a moment's rest, was distinct and fresh.

For the most part the trail ran over rocky ground overlaid thickly by fallen needles, but in places the ground was soft and Armand had not too much trouble in picking up the sign.

He waited for the others and then pushed ahead, Cleaver riding directly behind him, the rest strung out in a long, grim line. The trail was in most places too narrow for more than one man to pass at a time.

Finally Armand dropped back for a conference with Spain and Cleaver while several of his men pushed ahead, eager to win the promised award.

It should not be very long before they caught the escapees.

## CHAPTER THIRTEEN

Gordon Merrill heard the sound of the pursuit. Armand and Cleaver had too many men for quiet, and the ring of a shod hoof on stone carried a long way in the morning stillness.

Merrill stopped. The track they followed wound through heavy timber along the crest of a small hogback up the side of Dohne's Peak.

He had been carrying the girl. He now set her gently on her feet.

"What is it?" She caught the change in his manner, his sharpened attention.

He said tonelessly, "They're coming."

Harmony had the food sack, Clarence Donovan the rifle. The big cook dropped his burden and reached for the gun.

"Gimme that."

Merrill said quickly, "What do you think you're doing?"

"Go on," said the fat man. "Go on. I'll

stay here and give them something to think about."

"You're too fat for that kind of work." Merrill's voice was tight. "You take them on up. Keep off the trail and don't leave any more sign than you can help."

He did not speak to Clarence, but crossed and took the rifle from his hands.

"How many shells you got?" He was speaking to Harmony.

The cook looked at him, an argument forming on his lips, but Merrill cut him short before he could speak.

"Do what I tell you. They know we're up here and they're mounted, and there are probably a lot of them. It's only a question of time before they dig us out, unless I can lead them off."

"But how can you do that?" It was the girl.

He gave her a thin-lipped smile. "I know this territory, and a man on foot has a better chance in the timber than a man on a horse. Go with them."

Harmony reached into his sack and came up with half a dozen cold biscuits and a chunk of boiled beef. Silently he handed them to Merrill, then turned toward the girl.

She guessed his intent and said quickly, "I can walk."

He shrugged. He took a look at the sky, at the distant peak, to orient himself. Then he led the way off the trail.

Merrill had not waited. Already he was retracing the track toward a cut bank which rose fully fifty feet. He climbed it swiftly, the slope so steep in places that he had to pull himself up by the branches of the pines.

He gained the top and hurried along it until he found a place from which he could see the trail through a break in the thick growth.

There he squatted down. He pulled one of the biscuits from his pocket and gnawed on its hardness. He waited nearly ten minutes. They had been further behind than he had thought, and he breathed deeply in momentary relief. The ten minutes would give Harmony time to get well away from the trail. The cook knew the country well, and there was little fear that he would become lost in the maze of canyons and broken rockslides which scarred the mountain's breast.

It was a rough country. One surveying crew had lost its way when they had been running the main water ditch, and it had taken nearly a week to find the men.

Nor was he too concerned at his own situation. The bank on which he sat could not be reached by horse. They would be forced to dismount to dig him out, and on foot he was a match for twenty of them. In fact, in the deep timber their very numbers would work against them.

The first rider came into sight slowly. The trail was too narrow for them to ride abreast. Merrill waited grimly. He was watching for Armand, his brother, or Spain, but the first three men were strangers, and he did not want to let too many pass.

The fourth horse he killed with a single shot. The whipcrack of the rifle echoed back from the distant hills to set the woods alive with sound.

At once there was consternation on the trail, men shouting back and forth, the horses plunging.

His second shot knocked a man out of the saddle, and the high wild cry with which he went down added to the panic of his fellows.

Merrill was well-concealed. Half a dozen rifles cracked below, but their bullets searched through the trees without coming within fifty feet of him.

Then there was silence. No one was in sight below now, except the dead horse and the wounded man, who was trying to crawl to shelter, calling vainly for assistance.

No one came to help him, and Merrill let him go. He felt no animosity against these hired killers. His feeling was directed only against his brother, against Spain and Jean Armand.

As long as the others constituted no danger he had no desire to kill them, and certainly the wounded man represented little threat.

In fact he was an asset in that he would be a hindrance to the searching party. He was out of sight finally, dragging his useless legs, and there was silence on the hillside.

Then one of the men Merrill had let pass dashed back across his view. Merrill's shot dropped the horse, and the rider catapulted over its head to land rolling. Merrill kicked the dust beside him with a hurried bullet, but missed.

Silence fell again, then he heard Armand's voice.

"Merrill. Merrill."

He did not bother to answer.

"Come on down with your hands up. None of you will get hurt if you surrender."

They thought the others were with him. That was good. He grinned faintly, suddenly enjoying himself. This was a game he knew and understood. Usually he had been on the other side, the hunter rather than the hunted, but the tactics were always the same. If he could lead them enough of a chase he might break through and manage to cross the canyon. Meanwhile he would keep them occupied so that they would not hunt out the others.

He had often thought that the fox must enjoy the chase almost as much as the dogs who were attempting to corner him. But the fox, once cornered, had little defense, while Merrill had dangerous striking power.

He slipped fresh shells into the gun.

"Come up and get us."

His voice was a shout. It was not that he meant to dare them, but he wanted them to be sure that it was he who held the ridge.

There was movement in the trees below him. He could hear them calling back and forth but could make out only a few of the words. Then he heard Austin Cleaver hailing the two men still on the trail above him, directing one to circle up the ridge, to cut him off.

Merrill had been hoping for just this. He knew that he could not hold his present place for long. He had not intended to try. They could climb on either side of him, their movements masked by the brush and trees.

He fired two aimless shots in the direction

of Cleaver's voice, then slipped away and worked silently downward.

He wanted a horse. He had to have a horse to stand any chance of breaking through their lines.

There were sounds on both sides of him as his hunters made their climb up the face of the bank. He knew that they had to climb on foot. It was this that he counted on.

Once he caught fleeting movement on his right and froze motionless, holding his breath, his gun ready, but the man continued upward out of sight, and Merrill resumed his slow descent, angling along the edge of the trail.

He heard the stamping of the horses before he saw them. The flies were bad, and they moved restlessly under the torment.

One man still sat his saddle, staring upward at the ridge, holding the reins of his fellow's horse. Merrill was behind him and to the right. He stepped into the trail, saying softly, "Drop the rifle."

The mounted man stiffened. Then he let the rifle slide slowly from his hand.

"Now the six gun."

The Colt was lifted and let fall beside the rifle.

"Now get down, slowly."

The man swung out of the saddle obediently. Merrill was behind him with the speed of a mountain cat, and his swinging rifle barrel caught expertly along the side of the head. The man went over without a sound, and even as he fell Merrill had the horse's bridle before the startled animal could spring away.

The second horse he ignored. He stooped over the unconscious man, helping himself to the shells from his belt. Then he mounted and turned the horse down the trail.

He rode carefully, quietly past the dead horses which he had shot from above. He rounded a turn and found two of Armand's men with the bunched horses of the crew, held in a little clearing beside the trail.

They were not looking in his direction. Their attention was on the higher ridge, and he was on top of them before they were aware of his presence.

"Don't move, either of you."

They tensed but did not turn.

"Drop your guns and get over against that rock."

They obeyed silently. He stepped down and moved over. The horses were linked by a long picket rope. He freed it, then climbed back into his own saddle and began to haze the loosened animals down the trail ahead of him.

Behind him rose a burst of shouting. He glanced back. His prisoners had broken from the rock and were running toward their fallen guns.

He sent two quick shots and saw them leap for cover, then he was around a twist in the trail, hidden from view.

The free horses, spooked by the shouts, had lunged into a run. They held together for a few hundred yards, hemmed in by the fence of trees on both sides of the track, then as they reached a small meadow they scattered like quail, a long buckskin holding the trail alone, galloping on ahead.

Merrill was satisfied. He had gained precious time, for it would take Cleaver's killers hours to round up the scattered mounts, and he was drawing them away from Mary Campbell and the others on the mountain.

He eased the horse, conscious of the treacherous footing of the rutted way. A lame animal would be little good to him. He still faced the problem of trying to cross the canyon.

Behind him the pursuit streamed down off the ridge, shouting angrily as they came. The man at the upper end found his partner unconscious where Merrill had left him, but was lucky enough to catch the freed horse grazing nearby.

He hurried down to the others, where Jean Armand pre-empted the animal and took off after Merrill, leaving the rest to follow afoot.

When Armand reached the little meadow three of the mounts Merrill had freed had wheeled and remained there. The mine police chief roped them, snubbed them to trees, and then swung back to report to Cleaver, hauled a man up on his animal's rump, and galloped him again to the meadow.

The group on foot joined them, and within the hour they rounded up six other horses. It still left half a dozen men afoot and two wounded to look after.

Cleaver and Spain and Armand squatted in the shade of a huge tree and held a council of war.

"Merrill's free," Armand said, "but those with him are somewhere on this mountain. They have to be."

"Unless he circled back with the horses we haven't found and picked them all up."

"He'd have plenty of trouble. Aside from this trail it's rough going on this side. A man might be able to make it, but leading four horses would be next to impossible. I'd say they're around here someplace."

"They weren't on the ridge." George

Spain sounded positive. "I looked for sign. I found where Merrill had holed in behind some rocks. The empty cartridge shells were there, but there wasn't a mark that anyone had been with him."

"He probably circled," Cleaver said thoughtfully, "and they can't do us much harm as long as they're on the mountain."

"They might climb over and go back to Dayton."

Cleaver nodded. "They might, but that's going to take them two, three days. And you can't tell, they might run into someone and talk. George, take three men and see if you can pick up their trail. Jean, you've got to find Merrill, make certain he doesn't cross the canyon.

"I'll take the boys without horses and the wounded through the tunnel. If they do manage to get over the top, I'll be in town waiting for them."

He rose and walked away.

George Spain shrugged. "It's a waste of time hunting for Harmony and the girl. Merrill's the key."

Jean Armand did not deign to answer. He was already striding toward his horse.

# CHAPTER FOURTEEN

The cave was far from large, but it was dry.
The powdered sand floor was soft and held
a warmth which was a boon to Mary Campbell's back.

Actually it was not a cave at all but rather
a depression beneath an enormous rock.
The rock was so large that two trees, each
over a foot in diameter, grew on its top.
Park Campbell sat cross-legged beneath
the outer lip of the rock, gazing off across
the box canyon at nothing in particular.

The cave was halfway up the canyon wall,
and Harmony had stumbled on it by sheer-
est accident. He had been climbing, trying
to find if it were possible to scale the wall in
case of need, and he had dragged himself
around the bowl of a wind-canted tree and
seen the opening under the great stone. It
was well masked by brush, and he had
almost passed by, but as he tried to pull
himself up his arm had pushed the brush

aside and revealed to him a space eight feet wide and more than six feet in depth.

He bent the bough away and saw that the opening was clean and knew that it would afford them shelter for the coming night.

His charges were waiting for him beside the stream that trickled in a tiny silver ribbon across the stony floor of the little canyon. He dropped back down, told them of his find, and helped the girl to make the ascent.

She was exhausted by the time she reached the rock and crawled in under its guardian edge, and she lay, sinking into a half daze, barely conscious of what went on around her.

One of Harmony's few virtues was his cleanliness, and he set about tidying the cave as if it would be a permanent home. He brushed out the leaves and twigs deposited by the eddying winds in the corners of the cave, arranged their meager supply of food in a neat row on the folded sack, and carried the single cooking pot that he had included down to the creek, filling it with fresh water. Then, taking Clarence Donovan with him, he went back down to the entrance of the box canyon.

From the moment they had turned into it he had made his companions walk in the running water to cover their passage. Now as they came out of it he and Clarence Donovan moved out along the trail for nearly a mile, consciously leaving footprints in every soft place, breaking branches from the bushes in a deliberate attempt to mislead their pursuers.

George Spain found this blaze an hour later. He was not the woodsman Jean Armand was, but he had been reading sign for most of his life.

The trail led directly up the shoulder of Dohne Mountain toward the bare rocks of its blunted peak. He urged his horse forward, the two men with him staying close behind. He expected to catch the fugitives at every turn, but suddenly he realized that he had seen no sign for a good quarter of a mile.

He halted, dismounted, and searched the ground. There were deer tracks and nothing more. Even the deer sign was at least a week old.

Cursing silently, he turned, retracing his course on foot, leading his horse, his quick eyes taking in every detail of the side trail.

He found where the cook had left the decoy track and turned into the timber. The blaze was not as plain here, but there was a scar in the dust of the bank where Clarence

Donovan had slipped as he climbed.

Spain left his horse with his men and went up the bank alone, finding a shallow mark in the thick carpet of needles that underlaid the trees, another, and yet a third.

He loosened his gun. He had no desire to walk into an ambush as they had with Merrill on the ridge. But he pressed forward through the belt of thick timber until he came out at the base of a great rockslide.

He stopped, staring at it in consternation. The slide was nearly a mile in width and perhaps twice that distance up the pitch of the mountain.

A bare, jumbled mass of broken stone. Here and there a stunted tree had found precarious footing among the lifeless boulders, but for the most part it was whitely barren, an enormous avalanche that had slipped down in some earlier age, cutting everything before it.

The sign Spain followed led to the edge of the rocks and disappeared among them. There was no telling in which direction the people he sought had gone. They might have followed its base to left or right. They might have climbed up the slide toward the mountain's crest. They might have turned downward to recross the trail up which he had come.

Harmony saw him when he appeared out of the edge of the timber. Harmony lay concealed in a clump of trees a thousand yards from where George Spain stood. Clarence Donovan lay at his side, silent, watching, nervousness making him sweat.

Harmony's voice was a mumbled whisper. "Relax, kid. He don't know where we are, and barring an accident he's not going to find us."

"But how do we get back to the cave?"

"We go over that." Harmony pointed across the slide toward a hogback that rose some three hundred feet, between them and the box canyon.

Clarence started to get to his feet, but Harmony pulled him down.

"We'll have to wait. I know George Spain. He's the stubbornest man God ever made, and he has the patience of a Sioux. We'll just sit quiet for a couple of hours and see what happens."

Nothing happened. Harmony was dying for a smoke, but he would not take the chance. The smell of burning tobacco can at times travel far.

The sun was already down, almost touching the mountain, when he finally rose, groaning as he stretched himself.

"This ain't no work for a fat man."

He started then, across the base of the rocks, picking his way with a strange, rolling grace.

Clarence followed. There was no grace in him. His feet had always been too large for proper use, and walking over the broken stones took both balance and practice. The boy slipped and fell twice. Harmony, whose patience at best was short-lived, swung around as Clarence drew himself shakily to his feet after his second fall.

"Kid, didn't they even teach you to walk?"

The hatred which he had been trying to crowd down ever since Harmony had appeared with the sack of food flared dully in the boy's breast, but he was too weary even to make a reply. He plodded on silently, doggedly, until they reached the far end of the slide. Then he sank down in the shadow of the trees.

Harmony was ruthless. "It will be dark in an hour. We've got to get over that ridge." He put down a big hand and hoisted the boy to his feet.

They climbed. At times the face grew so steep that they were forced to backtrack and try another way.

Darkness caught them still on the wrong side of the crest and added to their difficulties. Clarence Donovan felt as if his heart was three times normal size. He felt that it would swell until it burst his chest. His every inclination was to lie down, to sleep. He had not been in bed for twenty-four hours.

And then they reached the top, and Harmony called a halt. The boy sank gratefully to earth. He was dizzy, sick at the pit of his stomach, and on the verge of tears.

A match scratched, and he turned. Harmony had rolled a cigarette. In the tiny flare of light the boy saw his face and was shocked by sallow grayness beneath the flabby skin.

He realized then that the fat man was suffering as much as he, perhaps more. Harmony was carrying nearly three hundred pounds to his hundred and thirty. He said in his thin, high voice, "You must think a lot of Mr. Merrill to go through all this."

Harmony looked at him. The moon was not yet up, but the sky held a reflected light that allowed them to see each other without really being able to distinguish the other's features.

"There ain't nobody like Ghost Merrill."

"You known him long?"

"Since Bodie. I had a restaurant there, and the toughs wrecked the place and put me out of business. They'd have killed me that night if the Ghost hadn't walked in."

"What happened?"

"He shot two of them and the rest took off. Then he gave me a job, cooking at one of the company's mines. When he took over the Dayton Pit he brought me up here. I been here ever since."

"Think he'll get through?"

The fat man started to say yes. Then he changed his mind.

"It won't be easy. There's three men out there all would like to see him dead, and they got a lot of help. . . . If anyone can make it, Gordon will."

He squeezed out the cigarette coal carefully on a stone and rose heavily.

"Come on, young'un. It's downhill from here on."

Clarence Donovan found that going downhill could be more difficult than climbing. They slipped and slid, clinging to rocks and trees, hunting for the cave. They missed it and were compelled to go to the bottom of the box canyon, then work back up.

Park Campbell challenged them as they were about to pass the cave on their climb. They crawled thankfully into the opening and dropped to rest.

Campbell said, "I thought you were gone

for good. Is there anything left in that bottle?"

Harmony said, "When I get my breath." He sat for minutes, breathing noisily through his mouth. Then he asked, "How are you, Miss Mary?"

She answered from the rear of the cave. It was too dark for him to see her, too dark for him to see anything. He struck a match. He found a handful of leaves and ignited them in the cave's mouth.

"Get some brush, kid."

Obediently Clarence Donovan slid down the bank. He found some dead branches on a pine below and brought them back, breaking them into small lengths and feeding them to the fire. It blazed up, illuminating the interior of the cave.

Park Campbell said, "Is it safe?"

Harmony shrugged. "If they happen to be in this box canyon, no, but the last I heard of them they were working on up east. And we've got to have some hot food."

He turned to where the girl lay, noting in a quick glance her flushed cheeks, the almost luminous quality of her eyes, and knew at once that she was worse. He handed the kettle to the boy, saying, "I hate to ask it, kid, but we need fresh water."

Clarence took it and wiggled out past the

fire. Harmony moved to where he had arranged the food and began digging in the sand. He found the pint bottle where he had buried it. From behind him Park Campbell swore softly.

"If I'd known it was there . . ."

"Sure," said Harmony. "I didn't want you to know." He removed the cap. "One swallow now."

The hand with which Campbell took the bottle was not steady. He held it for a moment and then to his own surprise extended it back to Harmony.

"I don't need it."

"Go ahead." Harmony sounded disgusted. "Let's don't be heroes at this late date. We've got other things to do."

Campbell looked at him. He shrugged. He raised the bottle to his lips. He took one careful swallow and returned it. Harmony took an equal swallow. Then he re-corked it and tossed it carelessly against the pile of food.

Park Campbell said, "You'd better hide it again, when I'm not looking."

"No," said Harmony. "You won't touch it unless I offer it. I've learned that much about you."

Campbell gave him a quick, studying glance. He said softly, "I never appreciated you before, Harmony. It only goes to show that it is foolish to form quick opinions of people. You, sir, are a scholar and a gentleman."

"And you're crazy," Harmony told him. "I can hardly write my name."

He turned as Clarence came back with the pot of water. He found four tin cups which he had tossed into the sack, poured water into each of them, then put the pot on the fire to boil, adding a chunk of already cooked meat and three handfuls of beans.

Mary Campbell watched him from where she lay. She said in a weary voice, "Please, could I have some water?"

He picked up one of the cups and crawled over to her side, raising her head with a big hand which was curiously gentle and holding the cup to her lips. He noted that they were parched with fever, a little cracked.

She tried to drink greedily, but he restrained her. "A little at a time. There's plenty where this came from."

"I'm so tired."

"I know. I'll have some broth in a little while. Lie back and try to sleep until it's ready."

She thanked him with her eyes. She lay back, drowsily aware of their hushed voices, of Harmony setting out the cold biscuits and moving again to stir the stewing pot, then joining Park Campbell at the cave entrance.

"You know more about her than I do. How would you say she was?"

The hotel man shook his head. "I don't like the look of things. I wasn't going to say it, but she was spitting blood this afternoon."

Harmony did not know much about sickness, but he had seen a number of lungers in his time.

"I don't like it either. They say the mountain air is good for them, but we're pretty high here. I don't like the noise she makes breathing."

Campbell spread his hands. "There's not one thing we can do about it."

Clarence Donovan had been listening open-mouthed. "You mean she's going to die?" He sounded stricken. Suddenly he was seized with a wild rebellion such as he had never known.

"She can't." He thought he was shouting it at the top of his voice, but in reality he was whispering hoarsely to himself. "She can't. She can't. She's the only one who was ever kind to me in my whole life."

At the boy's words Harmony glanced quickly across his shoulder to see if the girl had overheard. Apparently she had not. Her eyes were closed and her face peaceful.

"Not so loud." He said it in an undertone. "I don't know, kid. I wish the doctor could see her."

Clarence Donovan was already sliding out of the cave. Harmony said sharply, "Where you going?"

"To bring the doc."

"Come back here, you damn fool. . . ." But he was talking to the night.

Cursing, the fat man crawled after him. Below him he could hear the boy slipping and lurching in the darkness. He started down, but long before he reached the bottom he realized the hopelessness of pursuit.

He stopped, calling sharply, but Clarence Donovan paid no heed. He was driven by a greater fear than he had ever known, a fear not for himself, but for the girl.

"She can't. She can't. She can't."

The words ran through his head over and over. His descent down the canyon side was fall, fall, and slide. Twice he came up against unyielding trees jarringly. Once he hit his head on a rock. But he gained the floor of the canyon at last and started down it at a half run, dreading that the cook might catch him and prevent his going.

He slowed finally and stood panting, fighting for his failing breath. Then he moved on, turning out into the trail. He had no real plan. He only knew that he must reach the tunnel, that he must go back through it and find the doctor.

The weight of the gun Merrill had given him was suddenly comforting in his pocket. He took it out, carrying it in his hand, for now that the first urgency of his fear for Mary Campbell had abated he became conscious of his old fears for himself. The night was dark, and it was the first time he had ever been alone in the hills after dark.

Sounds which he could not identify reached him, animals moving through the brush in their nocturnal sorties. He pictured mountain cats close behind him, waiting their chance to attack. He thought of bears and the stories he had heard of these monsters. Then his foot struck something soft, giving under his toe.

His cry as he leaped back rang out shrilly through the night, and his finger squeezed the trigger of the gun.

The recoil tore it from his hand, and he turned to run. His boot caught on a protruding root, and he went headlong, knocking all the wind out of his thin body.

He lay, unable to move, afraid to breathe, waiting for the unseen horror to strike.

Nothing moved. No sound reached him. Gradually it dawned on him that whatever it was, it was not going to jump on him.

He sat up slowly, his lungs still aching, and fumbled in the darkness for his fallen gun. He failed to find it and struck a match. The gun lay beside the trail. He scrambled for it, then turned and looked fearfully over his shoulder. He laughed in quick relief. His toe had swung against a prone horse, and he realized after a moment that it was unmoving, dead.

# CHAPTER FIFTEEN

Gordon Merrill was riding slowly along the canyon rim when he heard the shot. He had spent a thoroughly frustrating day, for he had failed to break through the line of riders that Armand had sent in search of him. Three times he had avoided capture by the merest chance, and it was only because he knew the country better than his pursuers that he was still alive.

They had turned him back at the bridge, and Armand's men coming up fast behind him had almost hemmed him in along the canyon's rim. He had broken through, killing one man and getting a bullet burn along his left shoulder in return.

He might have gone north, but in so doing he would have led them toward the box canyon where Harmony and the others hid. Instead he turned east, hoping to find a place where it was at all possible to get down the canyon wall. But as if they guessed his intent they had blocked that direction.

By four o'clock he knew that he could not break out of the trap before darkness overtook him. He was forced to go north. He found a thick stand of timber in a shallow draw. There he tied the horse without unsaddling it and crept forward to a small outcropping from which he had a view of the country below.

He lay resting, watching carefully. Three times he saw the hunters. They seemed to be maintaining a patrol along the canyon, riding back and forth as if they had given up hope of running him to earth and were contenting themselves with trying to keep him hemmed into the back country.

He was desperately tired. Hunger gnawed at his tight stomach, and he needed a drink of water. But he did not move. He had the stoic patience of an Indian, and he schooled himself to wait until a full hour after nightfall.

Then he went back to the horse and swung stiffly onto the saddle. He came to the trail which he had followed that morning, crossed it, and started for the canyon rim, proceeding as quietly as possible.

The shot brought him to an abrupt stop. He sat motionless, listening, feeling the quiver of the horse under him.

For an instant he thought he had been spotted and that the shot was directed at him. Then he realized that he had not heard the whisper of the bullet coming through the thick bushes, that he heard no movement.

He continued to sit where he was, every sense sharpened, knowing that whoever was in the bush to his left could not be a friend.

As nearly as he could pinpoint it the shot had come from the trail which he had crossed only minutes before. He hesitated, then turned his horse and rode back to the edge of the timber.

In the east a silver moon had crawled above the peaks. Under the trees it was still very dark, but the trail showed patches of light, and across one of these Merrill saw a tall figure flow toward him.

For a minute he did not recognize the boy. Clarence was carrying the heavy gun in his hand, looking fearfully right and left as he came.

Merrill said, "Hey, kid," and saw Clarence go rigid.

"It's all right. It's Gordon Merrill."

Relief rushed through Clarence Donovan. He let the hand holding the gun sag to his side.

"Gee . . ." He came on at a half run.

"You fire that shot?"

The boy nodded in embarrassment. "I fell over a dead horse. I didn't know what it was. I didn't think."

"Get off the trail. Someone else heard it, you can bet on that. What are you doing here?"

The boy told him in a spill of words, his voice cracking. "She's dying, Mr. Merrill. She's dying. I've got to get a doctor to her."

"Where are they?"

"In a cave up the side of that box canyon you told them to go to."

"All right. Get back up there. Tell them I'm bringing the doctor."

"But you gotta get away. You gotta get word to San Francisco."

"That girl," said Gordon Merrill, "is more important than all the mining companies in the world, than all the gold in California."

After he had said it the words echoed back through his mind. She was important to him, important in a way that he had never expected a woman to be important again. If she died because he had been so self-centered in his work that he had brought her with him into these hills . . . it couldn't happen again. He had taken Ellen underground, and she had died. Now, it was Mary Campbell.

He swung the horse around.

Clarence Donovan said, "Wait." The word was a hushed whisper.

Merrill stopped, and then he heard it. Horses were coming along the trail, coming fast.

"They've heard the shot." He hesitated for the barest moment. "Get back into the bushes, kid. Hide until they pass."

He jerked the horse about and headed for the bunkhouse above the drainage tunnel, not even waiting for an answer.

He had no clear plan of action. He only knew that he had to reach the tunnel, to find the doctor, to start him toward the box canyon. Nothing else mattered.

He rode past the ruin of the bunkhouse and along the haulage road to the tunnel mouth. The rush of sound from the falling water engulfed him.

Short of the tunnel entrance by a hundred yards he dropped down, pulled the saddle from the horse's back, and hit the startled animal across the flanks with his hat. It veered away, galloping back up the road.

Merrill could only hope that it would reach the side canyon in which the bunk-house stood and abandon the main road before the approaching riders reached it. He turned then, pitching the rifle after the saddle into the canyon. It was of no use to him. It would in fact hamper his efforts.

He pulled his six gun and began to run.

The water's noise covered any sound he made, and he was in the tunnel mouth before the guard, sitting with his chair propped back against the rock wall, knew that anyone was within miles of him.

He jumped to his feet as Merrill ran in, stood for an instant thinking this was one of Armand's men, then reached for the gun at his hip.

He never got it clear of the holster. Merrill shot him twice. He did not stop to see if the man was still alive. He grabbed up the lighted lantern from the catwalk beside the guard's chair and ran on along the slippery boards.

There was no one else in the tunnel, and he reached the shaft without incident. He had forgotten his weariness until he began to climb the ladder, but by the time he reached the top his muscles ached and his fingers felt like curved claws.

The shaft house was empty. He blew out the lantern and placed it in the corner in preparation for his return trip, then he eased to the door and peered out at the pit.

This was the dangerous part, and he held the gun ready. The flaming torches eerily lighted the ground he must cross. If any of Cleaver's men were about he would be spotted before he could possibly get to the shading trees behind the mine office.

But he saw no one. The windows of the office showed dark and lifeless. The only movement he saw in the pit was that of the two monitor operators, both too much occupied with what they did to pay attention to anything else.

Merrill sprinted for the trees. He half expected to see someone come over the rim from the main street before he made it, but his luck held, and he dived into the shelter. He moved through the shadow until he had a full view of the length of the street. There were only a few people along the wooden sidewalks, and they were at the far end, clustered before the Pit saloon. In a spurt he crossed the street, rounding Ebell's blacksmith shop, into the alley behind.

Here he paused to catch his breath and consider. The light from the mine pit did not reach this far, and the mountain which overhung the town blocked out the moon. The alley was in heavy darkness, relieved only a little by a trickle of light from the saloon's rear window at the end of the block.

The question was, where would he find the doctor? And when he found him, would the man be sober? He had no idea what time it was, but he judged that it was not yet midnight.

Usually, unless he had changed his habits in the last few years, Parker would be in one of the saloons, probably the Pit, seated near one of the poker games.

The man never gambled, but with a whiskey bottle on the floor beside his chair he would sit quietly watching the play until his senses were so dulled by alcohol that he could no longer tell what was happening in the game. Then he would rise and move with extreme care from the building and along the street to the log structure which housed his office.

Here he slept, using the leather-covered operating table as a bed. Merrill had known this strange, friendless man for eight years. In that full time he had not seen him entirely sober, but neither had he seen him too drunk to ride to an emergency.

He stole along the alley, avoiding as best he could the piles of trash and rusting cans that littered its length. He came to the rear of the saloon. The small window that gave the alley its only light was set high in the wall. He reached up, hooked his fingers over the edge of the sill, and drew himself up until he could peer into the back room.

His brother sat at the single table with two men he did not know.

Merrill swore silently and dropped back to the ground. He had hoped that the room would be unoccupied, that he could slip into it and, unseen, survey the saloon proper.

He stood below the window, trying to hear what the men inside were saying, but the roar from the distant monitor drowned their voices. He was tempted to pull his gun, to charge into the room and take his brother hostage. The problem in this was that the outer door might be locked. He lifted the gun and moved quietly forward and tried the knob. It turned, but the lock was on.

He knocked loudly on the door. Nothing happened. He knocked louder, using the barrel of his gun. Still no one answered.

Exasperated, he dropped the gun into the holster and walked again to the window and drew himself up. The room inside was now empty. Apparently the three men had left it in the small interval of time between his first look and the time he tried the door.

Again he dropped to the ground. The window sash was set permanently in the wall and would not open. He stood waiting, deciding his next course of action. Then he went around the corner of the saloon and through the narrow passage which separated it from the building next to it. It was very dark in the passage, and there were no windows in either of the side walls.

At the street end he paused. Half a dozen men still loafed before the saloon. He could hear the mutter of their voices and dared not look around the corner for fear of being discovered.

And then he saw Jason Comstock. The old swamper had come out of the saloon to smoke, as was his custom. He leaned against the corner of the building, directly in front of where Merrill stood, drawing a blackened pipe from his pocket and packing it with black tobacco which he cut from a twist with a pocket knife.

Merrill worked close behind him silently. When he spoke his voice was pitched to carry above the monitor yet not loud enough for the men a dozen feet away to hear.

"It's Gordon Merrill, Jason. Don't move."

The old man had been tamping the tobacco into the bowl with a cracked thumbnail. He continued what he was doing and raised the pipe to his mouth.

"Yes, Ghost."

"Mary Campbell is very ill in the hills. I need the doctor. Is he in the saloon?"

"He's down at the bunkhouse. The men

you hurt are there. Cleaver brought them in."

"Where's Cleaver?"

"Standing at the bar."

"How many has he with him?"

"Four, and the place is full. Don't try it, Ghost. How'd you get back into camp?"

"Through the tunnel."

"Then go back as fast as you can. I'll try to get Parker down there. You meet him at the other end."

"Try. . . ."

"He's pretty drunk," said Jason Comstock. "I don't know whether he can climb down that ladder without falling off."

# CHAPTER SIXTEEN

Clarence Donovan crouched in the bushes to let the riders pass. In the darkness he could not be certain, but he thought he recognized George Spain and Jean Armand in the lead. There were eight of them, and he knew from the way they were riding that they had heard Merrill and were in full pursuit.

After they had gone he stood up uncertainly. Merrill had told him to go back to the cave, but there was nothing he could do there. On the other hand, they might catch Merrill, and he could be of help to the Ghost. He came out into the trail and started to run.

The gun in his coat pocket flapped against his leg and bothered him. He pulled it out and ran on, carrying it in his hand. Finally he could run no further because of his aching lungs and slowed to a walk, but he kept on plodding, and after a few minutes began to run again.

Just when he had decided that he would never catch them, the outline of the ruined bunkhouse rose out of the darkness, and suddenly he heard voices in the night.

Panic was an unthinking thing, gripping him, and he had a choking sensation as if his heart had leaped into his throat. He turned to run away and then caught himself, taking long, studied gasps of air in an effort to still the terror which held him.

Merrill was somewhere ahead. Merrill probably needed him. At least he had to find out. He left the trail and inched forward in the screening timber, searching a safe place to step before he trusted his weight on either foot.

He heard a horse snort, heard the clink of an iron shoe on rock, and knew that they were coming back up the side canyon toward the bunkhouse.

He stopped, waiting. The noise of the waterfall was dulled by distance to little more than a murmur. Above it he heard men's voices and had a sudden glimpse of two riders as they crossed a patch of moonlight, and he realized that they were leading other riderless mounts. They rode up to the front of the old log building and swung down. One man said heavily, "Let's get a fire going. It's near freezing."

Clarence Donovan had not been conscious of the cold. He had been too worried to notice much of anything, but a shiver ran up his back now.

The second rider said, "Better not. Armand said to keep out of sight and not attract attention to ourselves."

"Armand's a fool. What's he got to worry about now? They've gone up through the tunnel. I can't understand Merrill heading out that way. He must know that the town is blocked off."

"Maybe he didn't. We didn't see him go."

"Sure he did. Where else would he go? We found his horse down on the haulage road. He couldn't have climbed that bank, and he didn't go over the edge. It's straight down."

They tied the horses and moved on into the building. Through the hole in the roof Clarence caught the glint of light as they kindled a fire in the stove.

He eyed the horses nervously. They blocked the path before the house, and he wondered if he could get around them on the steep slope.

For suddenly he knew that he had to reach that tunnel, that he had to get back to Dayton. Merrill was in the town, and he couldn't know that the men had followed him through the tunnel. He had to be warned.

At about that moment Austin Cleaver learned that his brother had returned to town. He was standing at the bar in the Pit saloon, wondering how the hunt on the mountainside was coming when he glanced up at the backbar mirror in time to see Armand and George Spain come in through the door.

He straightened, all the worry which had been riding him lifting suddenly from his shoulders. Merrill was dead. He knew it as certainly as if they had shouted the news the length of the saloon.

Merrill dead. Ever since he could remember he had hated the thought of Gordon Merrill, for he had been very small when his mother began pouring her poison into his ear. It was Merrill and his mother who had blighted his life. It was Merrill who, by his very ability, had relegated Austin to the second place after their father's death.

He came away from the bar. He was certain that Merrill was dead, since he felt confident that his brother would never allow himself to be taken alive.

"Where'd it happen?" He asked it in a low tone as he reached them.

Armand said, "Where'd what happen?"

"Where'd you catch him?"

"We didn't."

He stared at them, his mind refusing to grasp the meaning of the words. He had been so very certain. Then as it dawned on him that Merrill was still alive, still uncaptured, his anger erupted through him. He seized George Spain by the shoulder, shaking him without being aware of doing so.

"Then what in hell are you doing here?" He screamed it loudly enough that everyone in the crowded room turned to look.

Armand said savagely, "Shut up, you fool."

The words cut through the red haze that had for a moment blanketed Cleaver's mind. His grip on Spain's shoulder tightened, but when he spoke he had his voice nearly under control.

"What did happen?"

"He came back here, so we came after him."

"Back here? You're out of your mind. How do you know?"

George Spain glanced around, noting the interest they were causing. "Let's go outside and talk." He led the way back to the street with Armand and Cleaver at his heels.

As they emerged, Jason Comstock turned the corner, returning from the bunkhouse to which he had accompanied Merrill. He stopped, then faded back around the corner, looking for all the world like an exhausted spirit in the darkness.

Once out of sight he turned and ran across the rough ground back to the bunkhouse, around and in through the kitchen door.

Doctor Vic Parker sat slumped in a chair at the kitchen table. Merrill was pouring coffee into him, saying tightly, "Come on, Doc. Sober up."

Parker groaned. "Let me die."

"I don't care whether you die or not, but not tonight."

Merrill glanced around as he heard the opening door, dropping the cup he held to Parker's lips and reaching for his holstered gun. Then he checked himself as Comstock came in. The old man was plainly agitated.

"They're here."

"Who are here?"

"George Spain and Jean Armand."

"Where?"

"They just came out of the Pit with your brother. They know you're in town. I heard them say your name."

Merrill swore. He turned back to look at the doctor, then he walked to the sink and from the pump filled a pitcher with water. He came back and poured it deliberately over Parker's head.

The doctor sputtered. Merrill cursed him. "You whiskey-laden hulk, drink this."

He retrieved the tin cup from the floor, filled it from the big coffeepot, and thrust it at the man. Parker tried to shove it away. Merrill drew his gun with his free hand.

"Drink that coffee or I'll kill you. You aren't any good to me unless you're sober enough to climb down that ladder in the shaft. Drink before I shoot you."

Parker stared at him resentfully. "I believe you would."

"You know goddamn well I would. Drink."

Parker drank. The hot liquid burned his lips, but every time he stopped swallowing Merrill waved the gun. He emptied the cup. Merrill refilled it. The doctor shook his head.

"Gimme some milk. Lots of milk."

Merrill jerked his head toward the big ice chest. Jason Comstock scuttled over and opened the massive door. One whole side was filled with large chunks of ice cut in the high mountain lakes during the preceding winter. Sawdust still clung to the white surfaces, for they had been hauled up from the ice house that night.

There was a gallon milk can in the other side. Comstock carried it back to the table. He pulled off the cover and motioned for the cup. The doctor waved it off.

"Gimme that." He lifted the can between his unsteady hands and poured it into his throat. Milk ran down on both sides of his cheeks, but he took no notice. The chill liquid cleared his head as the coffee had not done. He set the can back on the table and stood up uncertainly. He shook his head.

"Bring me a towel."

Comstock jerked a dish towel from the rack beside the sink, and Parker scrubbed the milk and water from his face and clothes.

"I'm not going to forget this, Ghost Merrill."

Merrill shrugged calmly. "Don't. Just get down through that shaft. When you leave the tunnel, follow the haulage road to the old bunkhouse, then take the old Dayton trail. There's a box canyon about five miles up Dohne's Peak with a stream running out of it. It's the first water you'll hit. Turn up that stream. They're in a cave in the north wall. Sing out when you come into the canyon. Tell them who you are. Harmony will hear you."

The doctor grunted.

Jason Comstock said, "I'll go with you." There was a dignity about the man that Merrill had never observed before.

"You can't walk that far."

"I walked a lot farther than that." Comstock glanced at Merrill. "What about you? They know you're in town. They'll make certain you don't get out."

"I'm not going to try to get out," Merrill told them. "I never was much good at running. I never learned how."

"They've got twenty men."

He wasn't worrying about the twenty men. They did not count. There were only three who counted, Armand, Spain, and Austin Cleaver. He'd wait his chance until he could face one or all of those three. After that, he would see.

He watched the doctor cross the kitchen and pick up his bag.

"You'd better take some cord to tie that to you. You'll need both hands on the ladder."

"I am perfectly capable of figuring that out for myself. The thing is, Merrill, there isn't much I can do for that girl. She should never have gone into the hills. There is only one treatment I know of for consumption. Rest and plenty of good food."

"What kind of food?"

"Milk. Eggs."

Merrill looked at Comstock. "Take some milk and eggs with you. I doubt if Harmony put any in his sack."

The old man nodded. He found an empty whiskey bottle on one of the shelves. He filled it with milk and thrust it into his pocket. Then he got a dozen eggs from the ice chest.

The doctor said, "You'll break them within half a mile. Here. Gimme." He opened his medicine kit, took out most of what it contained, reached for a couple of towels, and wrapped each egg separately.

Merrill watched him in amazement. The man seemed completely sober. It was as if he had not had a drink, and yet half an hour before he had not been able to stand upright.

Merrill said, "I'll try to draw them away from the pit so you'll have a clear chance, but they may have left guards in the shaft house or in the tunnel."

The doctor took a small pearl-handled gun from his pocket. He spun the cylinder, then replaced it.

"We can handle it. Come on, Comstock."

They moved toward the door. Merrill gave them time to get a hundred feet from the building, then he followed. He did not want to get too close. If he ran into the expected fight he wanted them in the clear.

He eased out into the night and stopped.

Curiously he was nervous. He had walked the dark streets of a hundred such towns, knowing that death might lurk behind any corner, and had never known fear.

But for some reason it was different tonight. He was surprised that he wanted to live, at least to live long enough to be certain that Mary Campbell was all right.

It was a new thought and brought a sardonic twist to his mouth. The irony of it, that he should become interested in a woman when the odds were stacked impossibly against him.

He had no illusions about his own prowess. He knew that much of his earlier success in ridding the mining towns of the undesirable elements had been because the men he faced had very little to fight for. It had been easier to swallow their pride, to mount a horse and ride away than to stay and fight him.

The men made the difference. The men who sought him tonight hated him with a deep personal bitterness accentuated by the high stakes for which they played. None of them would run in fear of him. They would stand and fight with the ferocity of wolves.

He reached the corner and paused to stand in the dark shadow of a store's wooden awning, looking up the length of the main street until it ran into the pit at its far end.

The doctor and Comstock had separated. He guessed that they had decided their movements would be less suspect if they were not together. As he watched he saw two men step from the shadows, stop the doctor, and apparently question him. With relief he saw Parker move on afterward.

He judged that Armand had ringed the town, that if he tried to break out of the small canyon occupied by Dayton he would be stopped before he could reach the surrounding brush. He looked back at the street and saw something he had not noticed before. The men who had stopped the doctor were moving slowly toward him, pausing at one building and then the next. Across the street were two more men. He had not seen them in their shadowed path, but they were keeping abreast of their fellows, searching the buildings on each side.

It was reasonable that there would be men combing the alleys behind the stores with a like thoroughness. He turned, glancing along the street the other way. Men were moving slowly up from the livery. Soon they would reach the corner at which he stood. He was in a tightening box.

He thought quickly, reviewing in his mind

216

the buildings which the town contained, measuring them in his memory as possible hiding places. There were only two that rose more than one story, the hotel and the building where Cleaver maintained the central offices of the mining company.

He could reach neither of them. The searchers had already passed both structures. He looked back. He had to decide in a hurry, and there was only one way to go. Up.

# CHAPTER SEVENTEEN

Without a light the trip through the tunnel was a nightmare for Clarence Donovan. He crept along, one hand clutching his gun, one feeling along the slimy wall.

The endless rush of water in the channel beside him created a sense of complete silence, of his moving in a timeless vacuum, and he walked with an increasing terror that he might bump into a guard in the darkness.

But he finally found the ladder and, thrusting his gun into his pocket, began to climb. Actually he found it easier to go up than it had been to descend. Far above his head there was a faint glimmer. At first he thought it was a light in the shaft house and feared that a guard had been stationed there to forestall him, but as he came nearer and nearer to the ground level it became obvious that the glow came from the flaming torches outside, shining through the window.

He reached the floor with a sigh of relief and climbed over the edge, staying on his hands and knees for a long moment, resting. Now that he had returned to Dayton he did not know what to do next. Fear and uncertainty again had him in their grasp. He dreaded having to step out of the shaft house into the glare of the leaping torches. He pictured in his mind's eye all of Armand's police gathered in a tight circle, watching the approaches of the pit.

And then he saw the door move and his breath stopped. He had heard no warning sound above the roar of the monitor. He was immobilized on his knees. It never occurred to him to reach for the gun in his pocket.

The door swung wide, and he found himself staring into the rectangle of yellow light. Against it the doctor's square body was a bulky silhouette, blocking out most of the glow.

The light from the window showed Parker the boy crouching near the ladder well. The doctor's nerves were at razor edge, and he did not at once identify the huddled figure. His hand swept toward the gun deep in his pocket, then he saw the white face and stopped, and relief made his voice rough.

"What the hell are you doing?"

Clarence Donovan got slowly to his feet, swallowing, not knowing quite what to say. Parker saw the hesitation.

"Merrill said you went back to the box canyon."

"You saw him? He's all right?"

"I saw him." The doctor's voice was dry. "And if you call being hunted down like a cornered rat all right, then he's all right."

"They haven't got him?"

"Not yet. At least I haven't heard any shots. But it won't be long." He crossed to the shelf, got a miner's lamp, and lighted it.

"Where is he?"

"Last time I saw him he was in the bunkhouse, but I don't guess he stayed there. Why?"

"I gotta find him. I gotta help him."

"You ain't going to be of any help," said the doctor. "No one is. Ghost Merrill's not going to come out of this one, and I'll lay you odds. He may take some people with him. I hope he does. I hope he gets that no good brother of his first, but the Ghost's finished."

The boy did not answer, and Jason Comstock chose that moment to come in through the door. Clarence Donovan stared at the old swamper in surprise but did not speak, for the doctor was saying, "You get stopped?"

"Sure." The swamper chuckled. "I told them that Cleaver sent me down here with a message." He grinned wickedly. "Sometimes, Doc, it pays to have a bad reputation. I just pretended I was drunk. Nobody ever worries about a drunk as long as he's quiet."

The doctor grunted. Comstock turned his attention to the boy.

"What's he doing here?"

"Trying to be a hero. Get back down that shaft, kid, before you get your fool brains blown out."

"No." Clarence moved toward the door.

The doctor reached out a hand to stop him. With surprising energy Jason Comstock shoved it aside.

"Let him alone. It's the first time the kid ever had a chance to do something. Don't knock it down. He's got to find himself."

"He'll find himself dead."

"There are times when it's preferable to be dead." The old man spoke with quiet bitterness. "Let's get going, Doc, there ain't anything either of us can do here."

He walked to where the end of the ladder extended above the shaft head, grasped the top round, and stepped across. After a moment Parker followed, leaving Clarence Donovan alone with his thoughts.

For all his resolve the thoughts were not happy. He stood for a long moment where he was, then thrust his hand into his pocket and clasped it around the gun. Then he walked slowly to the door and peered out.

He saw nothing to alarm him. It was an average evening in the pit. The two operators were just finishing another undercut. Even as he looked, the earth above cracked and came down with its accustomed thunder.

Clarence chose this moment to leave the shack. He did not run. He felt that he would be less conspicuous if he walked as casually as usual. He did not walk directly across the pit toward the town. He headed for the pit office.

It was dark, with no sign of life about it. He stood in its shadow, considering, debating whether to run for the trees that had served him before or cut across toward the street, less than three hundred yards away.

He started over the intervening ground, forcing himself not to hurry, keeping his head down, hoping that even if he were observed he would be mistaken for one of the workmen.

It was late. He had no idea what time it was, but he was certain that most of Dayton's ordinary citizens would be in bed. It was the mine police he had to fear.

He reached the small embankment at the rim of the pit and came up over it, looking down the rows of buildings as they ran away from him along the shallow canyon.

"Where you going, kid?"

There was the hot, dusty taste of shock, of fear, in Clarence Donovan's mouth. He fumbled for words and found himself incapable of speech. He did not even turn. He stood motionless, hearing the crunch of the man's boots on the loose gravel as he moved up behind.

"Where's your gun?" The man had noted that he wore no holster.

Still the boy did not answer. A rough hand came out, running over his pockets, and his captor grunted as he found the weapon. He took it roughly, grabbed Clarence by his bony shoulder, and spun him around.

"What's the matter, kid? You used to know how to talk when you were kitchen help in the bunkhouse."

Clarence found his voice. "I can talk."

"Then tell me where your friend Merrill is hiding. He's worth a thousand dollars to me."

"I don't know."

The blow was backhanded, across Clarence Donovan's mouth. He knew the salty taste of blood from his broken lips. His head jerked back, and he looked around for a place to run. A voice behind him said, "What's going on?" and a second guard came up.

"It's the kid from the boardinghouse, the one that was with Merrill."

The second man sucked his breath. "Where'd he come from?"

"Back through the tunnel with Merrill, I guess." He shoved the purloined gun in his pocket and grabbed a handful of Clarence's shirt, jerking the boy forward until only inches separated them.

He was a big man, in his early thirties, with a dirty, two-day growth of beard. He had already killed three men in his short life.

"If you know what's good for you you'll speak up. We've got this town bottled. A mouse couldn't get out of it if we didn't want it to. Where's Merrill hiding?"

"I don't know."

The man thrust him backward to arm's length and used his free hand to hit Clarence directly in the nose. The nose broke, crushing under the impact.

Clarence cried out involuntarily. Tears leaped to his eyes, and he tried desperately to wrench away, but the man's fingers were too strong.

"Talk, damn you."

"I don't know. I don't know. I don't know."

"You better find out quick. I'm going to break your fingers, one at a time."

"Gault. Hey, Gault. Where are you?" It was Jean Armand's voice, calling from the other side of the street.

Gault swore. He had hoped to capture Merrill before Armand realized that he had found the kid. He wanted the thousand dollars promised by Cleaver, wanted it for himself.

"Over here."

Jean Armand came out of a store building and squinted across. The torch glow from the pit came up over the embankment to cast a dim light at this end of the street.

"Who's with you?"

"Tom May and the Donovan boy."

Armand's voice quickened with excitement. "Where'd you find him?"

"I think he was hiding in the pit office. At least he just came out."

Armand crossed the roadway. He looked at Clarence Donovan's battered face without surprise.

"Where's Merrill?"

Clarence's hands were cupped over his bleeding nose. He spoke through them.

"He went back down the tunnel."

It took all of his courage to say it. His fear of Armand was a devouring thing, threatening to consume him. But he had to rescue Merrill. He had to stop them from searching the town.

Armand said in a silky voice, "Lie to me again and it's the last talking you'll ever do. Where is Merrill?"

"I tell you he went down the shaft." Out of his desperation, out of his need to prove to his tormentors that he was not lying, he told a half truth. "He came to get the doctor."

"He did what?"

"He came to town to get the doctor. Mary Campbell is sick. I guess she's dying."

Armand swore softly, not knowing whether to believe the boy. Gault was staring.

"Say, the doctor came by here a little while ago. I stopped him. He was pretty drunk."

"He was just pretending," Clarence Donovan said. Now that it looked as if they believed him he found that he had an inventive ability. "He was pretending so you wouldn't keep him from going. So was Jason Comstock."

"The swamper? What's he got to do with this?"

"We sent him to get the doc. We hid in those trees over there and I went down the street and found Comstock, then I took him back to Merrill. That was before you came up through the tunnel." He was talking directly to Armand.

The mine policeman was baffled. He could not make up his mind whether the story was true. It had the ring of truth, and the timing was all right. He looked at Gault.

"Did you see Merrill cross the pit?"

The man said, "You know I didn't."

"Could he have, without your seeing him?"

Gault hesitated. "Well, it's possible, while we were searching this end of the street."

"Did you see Jason Comstock?"

The man nodded.

"Did he cross the pit?"

"Yes, he did."

"Go to the shaft house?"

"I don't know where he went. The old bum is always wandering around. Who pays any attention to him?" Gault was on the defensive.

Armand said to Clarence, "Come on, kid, we're going to find out about this." He took the boy's arm. "You two make certain no one else goes into that shaft house. The chances are that this kid is lying, that Merrill is still in town. If he is I don't want him slipping away."

He led the boy down the embankment and along the street.

Gordon Merrill saw them coming. He had climbed to the roof of the hardware store and crouched behind its false front, watching the street below. He had reached his spot just in time, for even as he climbed he could see them searching the building three doors away.

The spreading light of the pit's torches enabled him to follow most of the action below him. Cleaver's men had finished their search of the town and were now gathered in a tight knot before the Pit saloon, apparently discussing him.

It was toward this group that Armand led the boy, and Merrill had no difficulty in recognizing the tall, gawky figure. He cursed softly to himself. He had not counted on this. It had not occurred to him that Clarence was not already safe with the others in the box canyon.

George Spain was talking to the mine police. He turned as Armand came up, saying in surprise, "Where'd you find him?"

Armand told him. "The kid claims that Merrill got back down the tunnel."

"How could he?"

Armand shrugged and repeated Clarence's story. "It's possible. Gault was careless. At least the doctor and Comstock apparently went down."

Spain said, "To hell with them. We'll round them up later. Let's find Merrill. Send half a dozen men back through the canyon. Tell them to check the horse guards and count the horses. If Merrill's stolen another one we're in trouble."

Armand nodded. He selected half a dozen men and gave them their orders curtly. "One of you tell Gault to go over to the shaft house and stay there." He did not wait for an answer, but pushed the boy into the main room of the saloon. George Spain followed, nodding toward the closed connecting door of the back room.

Armand piloted the boy ahead of him down the length of the saloon. The place was nearly empty, but a few men still lingered at the bar, interestedly aware that something out of the ordinary was afoot.

They watched silently in the backbar mirror as Armand passed, noting the boy's bloody face, but none of them so much as turned their heads. No one wanted trouble with the mine police.

Armand opened the door, and Austin Cleaver, who had been writing instructions to his San Francisco brokers, raised his head. At sight of the boy he half rose, then settled back.

Armand did not wait for his chief to speak. He said, "The kid says Merrill got away again, through the tunnel."

Cleaver sat studying the boy. His voice was pleasant as he said, "Let's see how he stands pain. Come here, boy."

Clarence Donovan did not move. Cleaver brought a cigar slowly from his vest pocket, lit it deliberately as if his only interest at the moment was in getting it to draw thoroughly. Then he took it from his lips, letting the smoke curl up around his face.

"I said to come here."

Still the boy did not move. Armand caught the back of his coat collar and shoved him forward until his flat belly was pressed against the table's edge.

"Put his hand on the table."

Armand lifted Clarence's right arm and laid the hand palm down on the felt cover. Still deliberately, Cleaver brought the coal of the cigar down on the back of the hand.

Clarence Donovan shrieked. He fought to free himself. He was not strong enough.

Armand held him like a vise. He shrieked again.

"Tell the truth." Cleaver's voice was without the inflection of any emotion. "Tell the truth or I'll burn clear through that hand."

# Chapter Eighteen

As soon as the boy disappeared into the saloon Merrill began to ease back across the store's flat roof. He did not know how he could accomplish it, but somehow he had to get Clarence Donovan out of their hands.

He paused before he reached the edge, dropped to his hands and knees, and crawled on until he had a view of the alley.

The light from the distant torches was not strong enough to give full vision, but with the help of the moon it showed him that the center of the trampled strip was empty.

Men could be lurking in the deep shadows along the rear of the buildings, but that was a chance he had to take. He swung over the edge and dropped lightly to the ground, standing tensely for a moment, his eyes searching the block ahead for movement or sound. There was none.

He stole forward then, gun in hand, keeping as much as possible out of any area of light, and he had nearly reached the saloon's rear door when the boy's first shriek beat out above the monitor's blanket of noise.

He stopped abruptly, then as the shriek came again he ran forward. He did not waste time in trying the doorknob. He put the barrel of his gun against the lock and pulled the trigger twice.

The heavy slugs literally tore the catch from the spintered wood. He kicked the door wide, diving through it, counting on surprise to protect him and give him an advantage.

George Spain was standing just on the saloon side of the inner door. One of Merrill's bullets crashed into the partition below his knee. He stared down in mute surprise, then as the second shot resounded he pulled his own gun, flinging the door open.

Jean Armand had one arm about the boy's shoulder, holding him. His other clamped the wrist, forcing the hand on the table to motionlessness. He swung around in sheer instinct, pulling the boy with him, using the thin body as a shield.

Austin Cleaver sat at the table facing the rear door. He shoved his chair over backward, dropped to the floor, and clawed at his coat pocket for the small gun he carried there.

Merrill was in the outer doorway, his gun covering the room. His eyes took in the whole picture at a single glance, and he threw a shot at George Spain as the most dangerous at the moment.

The bullet caught Spain in his shoulder, spinning him about. He did not fall. He did not again try to fire. Instead he dove headlong into the saloon and ran across it to the front entrance.

In the rear room Cleaver got his gun free and fired, the bullet low, going between Merrill's legs. Armand, still clutching the boy tightly around the neck, was struggling to reach his weapon with his free hand.

Merrill did not dare fire for fear of hitting Clarence Donovan. He jumped the six feet that separated them, grabbed the boy, and yanked him out of Armand's arms with a sweeping gesture. He swung the heavy gun at the same time, clipping it down along the side of Armand's head, nearly tearing the ear from the skull.

Armand had succeeded in freeing his gun from its holster, but as he swayed from the force of the blow its weight slipped from suddenly nerveless fingers and clattered to the floor.

Clarence was flung to his knees by Merrill's wrench.

Armand shook his head, then dived at Merrill, locking his arms about the other's waist, tripping him with one foot behind the legs. They crashed down together, Merrill underneath, his gun flying from his hand and skidding across the room.

Gordon Merrill felt Armand's fingers at his throat, felt the tightening grip and knew that he was strangling. He tried to claw away the viselike hands without success. The mine policeman had a grip stronger than anything he had ever experienced. He had a confused look at the face above him and caught the flash of triumph, the urge to kill mirrored in the dark eyes.

In sheer desperation he seized the man's right index finger and pried it backward with the last of his fading strength. The bone snapped. Armand cried out wildly, cursing, but fought to hold his grip with his uninjured hand.

Merrill broke loose. He got one foot against the top of the overturned table and used the resulting leverage to roll from under his opponent, then went crablike after his gun. But Armand was on him again in a rush, and they locked in each other's arms, rolling and writhing.

Austin Cleaver climbed slowly to his feet. He ignored the boy crouched on hands and knees. He stalked forward deliberately toward the struggling men, his eyes intent, his purpose obvious. He only waited a chance for a clear shot to put a bullet into his brother.

Clarence Donovan watched him in fascinated horror, involuntarily shrinking back toward the wall. And then his moving hand touched Armand's lost gun.

He felt it, hesitated, picked it up. He straightened, staying on his knees, and, using both hands to steady the black weapon, shot Cleaver twice in the center of his back.

Austin Cleaver was dead before he fell. He fell loosely, everything collapsing at once. His weight carried him forward so that he dropped heavily across the two embattled on the floor.

For a moment both were too surprised to move. Then Merrill tore free and rolled away. He lurched up to his knees, facing the open saloon door, and through it had a view of Spain charging back in through the front entrance followed by half a dozen of the mine police.

He looked about quickly, saw Clarence, and yelled at him. "The door. Close the door."

He had no time to say more, for Jean Armand had pulled the knife from the case between his shoulder blades and was on his feet, circling Merrill, the knife held like a sword, the point outthrust and glittering in the yellow rays of the overhead lamp.

As Clarence slammed the door and jammed the thick bolt home, Armand leaped in catfooted. The knife licked out. Merrill side-stepped like a dancer and took the intended blow under his right arm, catching the man's wrist and locking it against his side.

For a long instant they stood thus, straining against each other, their strengths nearly equal. But Merrill had the advantage, because Armand could not use his injured hand effectively.

Inch by inch Merrill forced the knife hand down until the wicked blade pointed to the floor. He let go with the hand which had been holding Armand's shoulder and grasped the wrist, twisting it. Still Armand did not release the blade.

Then Merrill pivoted, brought the arm up and across his shoulder, swung, and threw Armand over his head.

Armand fell spread-eagled. Merrill jumped for the gun that Clarence Donovan had dropped when he ran to the door. He scooped it up and straightened in one fluid move, expecting Armand to be charging him, then stopped in surprise. Armand had not stirred.

Merrill wiped his mouth with the back of his free hand. He was so tired that it was great effort to cross the room. He came above Armand and prodded the mine policeman with his toe.

Armand lay quiet. Merrill bent slowly, expecting a trick, holding the gun ready. He grasped the shoulder and turned the man partly over. The knife had been driven to the hilt in Jean Armand's stomach.

Merrill stared at it with unbelieving eyes. Then he was brought up again as someone hit the connecting door heavily from the far side. Automatically he put two shots through the panel, then he turned, caught Clarence Donovan by his arm, and, shoving him ahead, dashed through the door to the alley.

"Run for the pit, kid."

The boy needed no second urging. He raced away, his long legs distancing Merrill without effort. Merrill followed wearily. His muscles had little resilience, but he forced his tired legs into a half run.

He had covered half a block when Spain's men burst from the saloon's rear door. He turned, threw three shots after them, driving them back, paused to reload his gun, and ran on.

He ducked from one shelter to the next, pinned down at times for a moment, then dashing to the next building. Twice he stumbled over rubbish and fell. There was an unreality about the whole passage, for the howl of the throbbing monitor was heavy in the narrow alley and made it hard to hear even his own shots.

He paused still a hundred feet from the alley's mouth, wondering if he would ever make it. He looked back. A man was running toward him up the littered way. He had not realized that the pursuit was so close.

He fired and fired again. He saw the man drop. He continued to stand a moment, studying the deeper shadows. Then seeing no movement, he ran on again.

His one idea was to reach the shaft house, to try to get down to the tunnel before they caught up with him. He came to the last building and veered around the corner toward the pit.

And then he stopped. Clarence Donovan, whom he had hoped was by now safely in the shaft house, was crouched under the embankment, his back to Merrill.

Gordon Merrill glanced behind him, seeing a man appear from the alley, shot at him, and saw him duck back into cover. Then he raced across the street and dropped beside the boy.

"Why didn't you make for the shaft house?"

"Gault's there with another guard."

Merrill peered over the bank. He could see Gault leaning carelessly against the wall of the small building, and an exhausted numbness overtook him for a moment.

Jean Armand was dead. His brother was dead. But he had not won clear, and by the look of things they still stood little chance.

In a few moments the crowd in the alley would gather up their courage and charge in from the rear. He and Clarence might make a run for it down the street, but they would be quickly cornered.

He raised his head above the embankment and studied the pit. The two guards and the two monitor men were the only living beings in sight. He watched the latter as they slowly swung the huge stream of water against the face, and he knew suddenly what he had to do.

"Come on."

He was on his feet, scrambling over the bank, aware of Clarence Donovan galloping at his heels. He ran not toward the shaft house but toward the monitor mount, and they had covered half the distance before Gault and his companion spotted them.

Gault fired at once, but the distance was nearly two hundred yards and his bullet kicked up dirt in front of the running pair. The sound of the shots was lost in the thunder of the water. The men on the monitor faced away from Merrill and did not know that anyone was near them until he came panting to their side.

Gault and his fellow were running also, firing as they came. Whether they expected Merrill to try to cut across the corner of the face, to attempt escape up the mountain beyond the work area, he did not know.

He wasted no time. He swung his gun up and jabbed it into the back of the nearest man. The monitor operator turned, staring at Merrill in stunned surprise.

There was no use in trying to yell against the hissing water. It was impossible to be heard. With his free hand he gestured toward the edge of the pit. His lips formed the word, "Run." The man got the idea. He leaped down and started for the south rim as fast as his legs would carry him.

The second operator had swung around. He jumped at Merrill, both fists swinging. Merrill's gun came up and down in a chopping arc to clip the side of the man's skull, to drop him to hands and knees, where he stayed shaking his head for a moment, before crawling away.

Merrill forgot him. He dropped his gun into its holster, seized the handle bar of the monitor, and hauled it around.

Gault and his fellows were fifty feet away. As Merrill turned, one of Gault's bullets hit him in the shoulder. The force of the impact nearly knocked him flat. He clung to the handle bar for a moment, then he threw his weight against it and swung the cutting stream in a huge arc, away from the face.

The stream caught Gault and his companion in full stride. It tossed them backward fifty feet. Both were dead before they struck the ground.

Clarence caught the idea. He hurled his thin body against his side of the machine as the mine police, led by George Spain, came tumbling over the rim from the street and into the pit.

They were much farther from the monitor than Gault had been, but the stream cut along them like a scythe mowing down a row of straw. Stunned, some lay where they had fallen. Others tried dazedly to drag themselves off.

Merrill reached for the valve which shut off the flow of water. It took his and Clarence's combined strengths to turn it, choking off the aperture until only a trickle dripped from the blunt snout of the monitor.

The sudden quiet was deafening. Their eardrums had become so accustomed to the beating sound that now the silence was a pressure upon them.

Merrill was running forward, his gun again in his hand. Seven men lay prostrate on the bank. Two others had crawled over its edge. He came to Spain, now struggling weakly to his knees, snatching the gun from the limp fingers. Most of the others had dropped their weapons in their fall. All were too shocked by the bludgeoning of the water to offer any resistance.

People were beginning to appear from the hotel and the bunkhouse. Merrill motioned them forward. They came, hesitant, uncertain, and wary.

In incisive, short sentences he took charge.

"Cleaver's dead," he said. "So is Jean Armand. I am holding Spain for the sheriff. The rest of the mine police may leave town if they're able."

The merchants gaped at him. The workers from the bunkhouse took his leadership in stolid acceptance. The night had shocked them into unquestioning obedience.

Merrill directed them to carry the dead to the town's funeral parlor. Three who lived through the barrage suffered broken arms, and these he sent to the bunkhouse. He chose two workmen to guard Spain, although the man seemed to be hurt internally aside from the wound he had sustained in the saloon.

These orders out of the way, Merrill turned to Clarence Donovan.

"Come on over to the hotel and let me see that hand." He led the boy down the street and into the bright lobby.

The burn was a red, angry thing. He soaked the hand in warm water, covered it with sweet butter, and then bandaged it.

"That will have to do until the doc can look at it. We can't do much about the nose. It hurt?"

"Not so much now."

Merrill bathed the blood from the thin face. He poured a cup of coffee and brought bread and cold meat from the icebox.

"Don't eat too much at one time."

The boy looked away from the food, up at the man. "Let me look at your shoulder."

"Later. The bullet went clear through. It will be all right. I've got to start somebody with a wagon to pick up the others."

The boy stood up instantly. "I'd better go with them. I know where they are . . . or maybe you better go."

"I've got things to do. Go if you feel up to it."

The boy nodded vigorously.

Merrill said suddenly, "You're all right, Clarence. Don't ever tell me again that you haven't got guts."

Clarence Donovan opened his mouth to say something. He stopped. He could not find the words he needed. He turned and started for the street, carrying a hunk of cold meat in his good hand. He was crying.

# Chapter Nineteen

Seven hours later the fugitive party wound down the old trail and reached the bunkhouse above the tunnel's opening.

Harmony Jones rode in the lead carrying Mary Campbell in his huge arms. He stopped the horse beside the wagon and saw Gordon Merrill step out of the wreckage of the building and walk toward them. The wounded arm was in a sling, and he looked more like a ghost than ever.

"How is she?"

"Sleeping," said Harmony in a soft rumble. "She's just plain tuckered out. That's what the doc said."

The doctor had passed Harmony and swung down at Merrill's side. Merrill's eyes asked their question. Vic Parker shrugged.

"You never know in cases like this, but I'd say she has a better than even chance. That helps, that and her determination to stay alive, of which you are the major component. Now, you wouldn't happen to have a drink in your pocket in appreciation?"

Merrill's lips quirked tightly. He reached into his coat and found the flat bottle. The doctor took it eagerly. He pulled the cork, hesitated, then shrugged, and, walking back, offered it first to Campbell and then to Jason Comstock.

The swamper reached, then drew back his hand. Campbell said, "Don't be a darn fool. You earned it."

"I'll say he did," Parker grunted sourly. "Why didn't you warn me? There were eight mine police with those horses."

"How did you get through?"

The doctor grinned like an aging pixie. "We suckered them. They were in the bunkhouse, all but one. I sent Jason in. He said that Cleaver had sent him with a message. He got close enough to get the drop on the one outside, took his gun, then shoved him in ahead. I was around back. I poked my gun through the window and told them to throw their iron in a pile on the floor. They did it. Then we ordered them to mount up and ride out. They did that too."

"I know." Merrill's tired eyes held laughter behind the drooping lids. "They got to town about daylight. All the fight was out of them. They'd met Clarence and the rescue party on the road and heard about Armand's death."

He turned to the boy. "How's your hand?"

"All right. The doc said you did a swell job."

"Have any trouble coming out?"

The boy shook his head. "I wasn't even afraid. I got to thinking, all these years I've been scared and nothing much ever happened to me. Fear's a funny thing. You imagine all the bad that can happen, and you get afraid it will.

"I was afraid going through the tunnel. I was afraid running through the woods. I was afraid in the cave. But none of the things I was sure were going to happen did. . . ."

He broke off in confusion. "I guess I sound pretty crazy."

"Why not?" said the doctor. "You are. We all are. Mankind has been crazy ever since it stood up on two feet."

He moved on to Harmony, stopping beside the horse and holding up his arms. The big cook lowered the girl into them. She stirred, and her eyes fluttered open. She twisted her head and saw Merrill, and her lips curved in a tiny smile. Then the doctor carried her to the wagon, where Clarence had prepared a bed of saddle blankets.

Clarence untied the team and hopped to

the driver's seat. Parker climbed into the wagon bed beside the girl. Merrill swung up beside the boy, and the others mounted the horses to follow.

The train moved out, the iron tires of the wheels grinding over the rough stone road.

Clarence's mind still puzzled over its philosophical questions.

". . . And I was afraid she was going to die. You said she'd be all right. How did you know?"

Merrill looked unseeing over the sweep of the great canyon to their left. How had he known? And yet, he had known. It had to be that way.

He could not explain the knowledge to himself and therefore could not explain it to the boy. He was not a religious man. He had lived by his own code. But he had a sense of predestination, as if there was no escaping that which was written.

When Ellen had died he had felt his life completely finished. He had lived on, carried forward by his old obligation to Boris Trueblood and with no hope of any future for himself.

Mary Campbell had changed that overnight. He tried now to picture Ellen as he had pictured her so many times in his mind, but whether because he was bone-weary to the point of mental exhaustion or because he had a new vision interposed between them, the image had become blurred and indistinct.

"Will you get the stolen gold back?" he heard the boy say.

He nodded absently. The gold no longer sounded as important as it had.

"George Spain talked. He's badly hurt. His ribs were crushed and he's scared of dying. He told me where Austin kept the full records. I know exactly how much was taken, when, the names of the brokers who received it, the amount of stock they purchased, and the names it was purchased in. I think Trueblood's lawyers will have no difficulty in recovering."

"And are you going to run the mine?"

Merrill shook his head. "I'm going to take her to Denver."

He turned to glance at the girl, quiet in the wagon bed. Her eyes were closed, and he guessed that she had gone back to sleep.

"Denver?"

"They say it's the best climate, and they've had so many like her that the doctors are trained for it."

He caught the trace of disappointment on the boy's narrow face.

"You'll be going with us. If you're going

to be an engineer you need schooling."

"You mean that?" Clarence Donovan's voice rose like a surprised child's. "You aren't fooling me?"

"I'm not fooling you," Merrill told him, "but I may need you to help me convince her. Sick people are sometimes hard to convince. They feel that they're a burden. . . ."

"She'll go," the boy said with certainty. "She'll go with us. She'll listen to me. She knows that you aren't just sorry for her. She knows you need her as much as she needs you."

He gave Merrill a conspiratorial grin. "She told me so, before we left the cave."

We hope you have enjoyed this Large Print book. Other Thorndike, Wheeler, Kennebec, and Chivers Press Large Print books are available at your library or directly from the publishers.

For information about titles, please call or write, without obligation, to:

Publisher
Thorndike Press
295 Kennedy Memorial Drive
Waterville, ME 04901
Tel. (800) 223-1244

or visit our Web site at:
http://www.gale.cengage.com/thorndike

OR

Chivers Large Print
published by BBC Audiobooks Ltd
St James House, The Square
Lower Bristol Road
Bath BA2 3SB
England
Tel. +44(0) 800 136919
email: bbcaudiobooks@bbc.co.uk
www.bbcaudiobooks.co.uk

All our Large Print titles are designed for easy reading, and all our books are made to last.